THE INTEGRATED MAN

A JOURNEY THROUGH MASCULINITY, SHAME, AND FREEDOM

B ALAN BOURGEOIS

The Integrated Man
Copyright © 2025 B. Alan Bourgeois
All rights reserved.

This book is a work of fiction. Names, characters, places, and incidents are either the product of the author's imagination or are used fictitiously. Any resemblance to actual persons, living or dead, events, or locales is entirely coincidental.

No part of this book may be reproduced, stored in a retrieval system, or transmitted by any means—electronic, mechanical, photocopying, recording, or otherwise—without the prior written permission of the author, except for brief quotations used in critical reviews or scholarly articles.

For permissions, licensing, or bulk purchase inquiries, please contact:
Texas Authors Press
TexasAuthors.Press

ISBN: 9798293335152
First Edition: 2025
Printed in the United States of America
This book contains themes of personal transformation, identity reclamation, and self-acceptance. It is intended for mature readers due to thematic elements related to self-identity, internal conflict, and community dialogue.

Cover Design by: AI Generated
Interior Layout by: Texas Authors Press
Publisher: Texas Authors Press, a division of Texas Authors Museum & Institute of History, Inc.

For more information about the author's other works and upcoming events, visit: **BourgeoisMedia.com**

B ALAN BOUERGEOIS

STORYTELLING
LITERACY & HERITAGE

Thank you for purchasing this limited edition book, offered in celebration of the author's 50-year milestone. Proceeds from your purchase support the Texas Authors Institute of History, a museum founded by the author in 2015, dedicated to preserving the legacy of Texas authors.

https://TexasAuthorsMuseum.com

Part I: The Unshakable Man

Chapter 1 "The Sermon of Strength"	6
Chapter 2 "The Crack in the Mask"	11
Chapter 3 "Ghosts on the Pacific"	17
Chapter 4 "The Alpha Lie"	22
Chapter 5 "The Oil Can Files"	27
Chapter 6 "The First Dream"	31

Part II: Cracks in the Armor

Chapter 7 "Saboteur of Self"	36
Chapter 8 "First Night Jitters"	40
Chapter 9 "The Mask Breaks"	43
Chapter 10 "Confrontation with Mirrors"	48
Chapter 11 "Confession of the Cloth"	52
Chapter 12 "Choosing the Stage"	56

Part III: The Integrated Self

Chapter 13 "The Reclamation of Masculinity"	60
Chapter 14 "Backlash and Breakthrough"	64
Chapter 15 "Quiet Aftershock"	67
Chapter 16 "Letters from the Past"	70
Chapter 17 The New Sermon"	73
Epilogue	77
About the Author	80
Other Books by the Author	82

Part I: The Unshakable Man

Chapter 1
"The Sermon of Strength"

Derrick Maddox stood tall in the center of the mid-sized auditorium, its walls pulsing softly with the ambient lighting chosen by his design team. The glow was intentional—neither sterile nor over-the-top, but steady, masculine, grounded. A crowd of nearly six hundred men, spanning decades in age and a rainbow of racial and cultural backgrounds, sat in rapt attention. Each had paid good money for this seat, to hear Derrick deliver what many considered to be the gospel of modern gay masculinity.

He wasn't just another motivational speaker. He was the flag bearer of a movement—a reclamation project for men who were tired of being told their strength was a flaw, their discipline a disguise, their masculinity a political liability.

"Gentlemen," Derrick began, stepping forward with the grace of a practiced orator, his voice carrying with natural ease into the microphone pinned discreetly to his tailored lapel. "We've been told we must fit in a box, labeled by society and, just as often, by our own community. I'm here to tell you—masculinity is not a vice to be tamed. It is a virtue to be honored."

A murmur rippled through the room, the first subtle note of connection. Not explosive applause—Derrick's audiences didn't engage in that hyperbolic behavior—but thoughtful, approving nods. The kind that said: *Yes, this man speaks to my experience.*

Derrick continued pacing, the heavy wood floorboards beneath the industrial carpet softening his deliberate footfalls. His movements were precise—two steps, pause, shift his weight, meet someone's gaze in the third row, pivot, and deliver a hard truth into the open air.

"We've allowed ourselves to be caricatured," he pressed on, his voice tightening just enough to underscore conviction without tipping into aggression. "Turned into punchlines, entertainment for the masses—dancing mascots for straight amusement."

His left hand lifted in a small, open-palmed gesture, inviting agreement. A few voices murmured "yes" and "exactly" in quiet affirmation.

Behind him, the high-definition screen projected an understated visual—images of nature's raw, unfiltered strength. Majestic mountain peaks under dusky skies, a lone wolf staring directly into the lens, the rhythmic crash of Pacific waves against unyielding coastal cliffs. It wasn't gaudy or cliché—it was primal, real, elemental.

Derrick moved smoothly into the core of his doctrine. *Discipline. Dominion. Devotion.* Three pillars that had, in many ways, built his empire. Each segment of the talk peeled back layers for his audience, challenging them to cultivate their physical resilience, master their inner world, and remain steadfast to higher callings—whether those be fatherhood, entrepreneurship, spiritual enlightenment, or artistic creation.

He told stories of transformation. Men who had spent their twenties in perpetual nightlife, caught in the vortex of cheap dopamine and shallowness, who had emerged through Derrick's teachings to build disciplined, fulfilling lives. A former addict who reclaimed his health through martial arts. A drifting corporate manager who became a coach and reconciled with his estranged son. Men who stopped running from their masculinity and learned to wield it responsibly.

The crowd stayed with him—intensely focused, pens scribbling notes, eyes reflecting flashes of recognition and longing. Derrick knew how to read a room, and tonight was textbook.

The talk rolled on, meticulously designed to lead them up the slope of revelation and plant them on a plateau of inspiration. Every word, every pause, every gesture was deliberate. This was Derrick's domain—an ecosystem where he reigned supreme.

As the closing lines approached, he slowed his cadence, lowered his tone, and allowed for soft silence between statements.

"Masculinity is not the villain it has been portrayed to be," he said, his voice dipping into a velvet baritone. "It is not oppression. It is not toxic. It is creation. It is stewardship. It is power tempered with responsibility."

A standing ovation? No. But a rising sea of applause, respectful and powerful, swept the room as Derrick concluded. He smiled, bowing slightly, the applause washing over him like a practiced balm. He didn't crave the raw hysteria that other speakers courted. He preferred this: the reverence of men ready to listen, ready to follow.

Backstage, the atmosphere shifted. The brightness of the stage dimmed into the softer, muted tones of the corridor leading to the dressing rooms. Derrick walked with purpose but allowed his shoulders to drop a fraction. Julian, his young, efficient assistant, was waiting near the refreshments, phone in hand.

"Clean," Julian remarked. "No timing hiccups. I made notes on one slide transition, but otherwise—flawless."

Derrick took the offered bottle of electrolyte water, unscrewed the cap, and drank half of it in one go. The adrenaline was beginning its slow decline, and in its place, the methodical post-performance analysis took over.

Julian scrolled through his phone and flicked a notification open. "LA dates are locked in. Marriott Downtown, two-night series, live Q&A on night two. A few podcast slots lined up, gay press mainly. We're being selective about on-site media."

Derrick wiped his mouth with the back of his hand, his expression tightening subtly. LA. The name carried a sharpness, an edge dulled by years of avoidance but never truly forgotten.

"Venue?" Derrick asked, his voice clipped, neutral.

"Grand Ballroom, capacity seven hundred each night. You'll be headlining the weekend speaker lineup." Julian's voice carried no emotion, but the information felt like a slap.

The address blinked up from Julian's phone screen. Downtown Los Angeles. Eighth Street. Less than five blocks from where Derrick had once shimmied on a makeshift stage, chest hair puffed out over an ill-fitting sequin crop top, mouth painted firetruck red while swinging fake breasts fashioned from dollar store balloons.

The shift was subtle but immediate—Derrick's pulse picking up, grip tightening around the bottle until the plastic creaked under the strain. He forced his breathing to steady, fought the heat rising in his chest.

"Everything good?" Julian asked, casually glancing up. "Your post-event meet-and-greet starts in fifteen. Nothing too heavy, just a photo line and light chat."

Derrick nodded mechanically. "Fine," he said, but the word landed flat, brittle.

Julian didn't press further, returning to his screen, but Derrick's mind had already started to wander.

Images he hadn't summoned in years began swirling—glimpses of chaotic nights drowned in glitter and bad pop remixes, of crude cheers from packed crowds who adored the absurd spectacle he provided. The camp drag alter ego he had murdered, buried beneath years of discipline and polished branding, was clawing at the edges of his mind, resurrected by a single word: *Los Angeles*.

He adjusted his blazer in the dressing room mirror, smoothing out invisible wrinkles, focusing on his perfectly tailored reflection. But behind the impeccably groomed beard, the strong jawline, and the commanding posture, he could feel it—a crack, small but insistent, working its way through the walls of the image he had built brick by careful brick.

LA wasn't just another tour stop. It was a return to the killing field of his former self, to the birthplace of Dirty Divine and the Oil Can Oilers. And despite all his success, all his structure, all his carefully honed masculine essence... part of him wasn't ready.

Part of him was terrified.

He grabbed his phone, locked eyes with his reflection, and took a steadying breath. Fifteen minutes to recalibrate. Fifteen minutes to shove the past back into its grave.

With one last look in the mirror, Derrick turned sharply and walked out the door, his footsteps echoing just a little louder than before, the crack expanding, silent but undeniable.

Chapter 2
"The Crack in the Mask"

The afterglow of a successful night lingered as Derrick Maddox boarded his private shuttle back to the hotel, the bright city lights of New York casting long reflections against the tinted windows. Julian sat beside him, tapping through emails on his tablet, completely unaware of the quiet storm beginning to brew beneath Derrick's composed exterior.

The vehicle hummed softly, a high-end hybrid, smooth and silent on the road. Derrick appreciated the tranquility. In truth, he needed it. His mind hadn't quite settled since stepping off stage. The words, the applause, the nods of agreement—it was the fuel he lived for, and yet... tonight something felt different. An unshakable tightness wrapped itself around his chest, a premonition he couldn't quite name.

Julian broke the silence, his voice efficient and professional. "I've confirmed the next two engagements. Chicago next weekend, and then—" he paused, fingers scrolling through his tablet, "Los Angeles. The big one. Two-night series, Downtown Marriott."

Derrick stiffened before he could hide it. His hand, resting casually on his thigh, curled into a slow, tense fist. "Los Angeles," he repeated, carefully, letting the syllables settle on his tongue like a distasteful aftertaste.

Julian nodded, tapping a few more times, pulling up details. "Headliner for their annual men's leadership weekend. Capacity seven hundred each night, major gay lifestyle outlets already interested. LA Times *might* cover it, but we're focusing on targeted gay media, especially podcasts. They've allocated full branding rights, so your visual package will dominate the venue. Your name's already on their landing page."

Derrick's mouth felt dry. He took a slow breath, hoping to chase away the rising tension in his chest, but it was futile. The words *Downtown Los Angeles* had an entirely different weight in his world. They weren't just coordinates on a map—they were coordinates of his undoing, reminders of a life he had buried so deep it rarely stirred anymore.

"Projected attendance?" Derrick asked, keeping his tone clipped, professional.

"Sold out within forty-eight hours," Julian said, barely concealing his pride. "You've got a solid footprint there. Two Q&As, one exclusive VIP dinner, and the closing keynote. They also want you on *Modern Mindset,* a huge podcast in the LA queer community."

Derrick nodded, the motion tight and mechanical. He leaned back, closing his eyes, but that only opened the floodgates.

Memories seeped in like unwelcome intruders—bright neon lights, sweaty dance floors, cracked stages in seedy bars that reeked of stale beer and lingering cigarettes. Los Angeles wasn't the polished, modern metropolis he now visited for business. It was the city where Dirty Divine had been born in a haze of rebellion and desperation.

His eyelids squeezed shut tighter, but the images were already in motion. Twenty-four-year-old Derrick, or rather Dirty Divine, hoisting her balloon-stuffed chest in front of screaming drunk men, his chest hair puffing out proudly under a ridiculous bedazzled crop top. Smeared lipstick that rarely stayed within the lines of his mouth, boots that pinched his toes after three hours of high-energy parodies of pop anthems. Night after night of lewd comedy routines and gloriously offensive dance numbers. The crowd didn't care about the artistry—they wanted the absurd, the vulgar, the grotesque. And Dirty Divine delivered with gusto.

It was freedom, Derrick reminded himself bitterly. A chaotic, beautiful freedom that came at the cost of self-respect. He'd laughed back then, laughed until his ribs hurt, but every morning after was met with the hollow ache of knowing the world only valued him for the joke he made of himself.

A buzz pulled him out of the spiral. Julian angled the tablet toward him. "Draft post for socials. Want me to run with it?"

Derrick glanced at it: a sleek black and silver poster, his face stern and powerful above bold white letters—*The Uncompromising Man: LA Takeover, Two Nights Only*. The image of himself was perfectly curated—masculine, composed, a paragon of disciplined strength. The stark contrast to Dirty Divine's gaudy posters, which were likely rotting away on some forgotten Facebook page, stabbed at him.

He swallowed, voice tight. "Go ahead."

Julian's fingers flew over the screen, sending it out into the digital ether. Derrick leaned his head against the cool glass of the window, counting his breaths.

Back at the hotel, the suite was pristine, an impersonal haven of high-thread-count sheets and designer furniture. Derrick peeled off his jacket, kicked off his shoes, and paced. The floodgates were open now, and no amount of mental discipline was enough to stop it.

He wandered to the floor-length mirror, staring hard at his reflection. The salt-and-pepper beard was trimmed with military precision, his body strong beneath the tailored white dress shirt. Yet, beneath it all, he could still trace the ghostly outline of Dirty Divine, lingering just below the surface.

"Is this what you built it all on?" he asked himself quietly. *"A lie?"*

It wasn't a lie, he corrected. It was… survival. Back then, it had been necessary. A way to exist in a world that had no place for men like him—rough-edged, unfiltered, unwilling to perform femininity in polished, palatable ways. Dirty Divine had been his rebellion, his way of flipping off both heteronormativity and gay cultural expectations. But in time, it became a cage, a mockery that he couldn't bear.

And now… now he was something else entirely. Derrick Maddox, the man who told other gay men they could embrace their power, their masculinity, their leadership. He had clawed his way out of that world, built an empire on restraint, on dignity. But the crack… it was forming. He could feel it. Each breath in this pristine room tasted a little more sour, a little more counterfeit.

He sank onto the sofa, scrolling absently through his social media feed. His upcoming LA gig was already gaining traction. *"Finally, a voice for masculine gay men!"* read one comment. *"No more clown routines and sashaying nonsense,"* praised another.

Derrick felt something sharp twist in his chest. His own words, his own messaging, weaponized in ways he hadn't anticipated. He'd never told people to hate camp or femininity—he told them to honor themselves, to embrace balance. Yet the line had been drawn, the tribalism inevitable. Masculine versus effeminate. Respectable versus ridiculous.

And what would they say if they knew? If those commenters saw Dirty Divine in her chaotic glory? If they knew the foundation of Derrick Maddox's kingdom was once sequins, crass jokes, and foam-padded boobs?

He stood abruptly, moving to the minibar, pouring himself sparkling water over ice. The chill helped slightly, but the gnawing didn't fade.

His phone buzzed again—Julian.

"CNN declined, but two gay networks confirmed, and LA queer scene podcasts are fighting for a spot," the message read.

Derrick tapped a quick response, trying to silence the rising anxiety. His heart drummed too fast in his chest. He needed focus, clarity. He needed to bury this before it consumed him.

He sat at the small writing desk, laptop open, and for the next hour, Derrick crafted a masterclass outline for his LA appearance—leaning even harder into discipline, masculinity, and identity sovereignty. He'd reinforce his narrative, tighten his armor, silence the past with the force of forward motion.

But when he closed the laptop, when the notes were done, the tension hadn't eased. His gaze drifted to the floor-to-ceiling windows, the New York skyline glittering against the night sky. And in the glass reflection, for just a second, he swore he could see a flash of blue eyeshadow and a crooked, mischievous smile staring back.

He blinked it away, pressing his temples firmly with his fingertips.

LA was two weeks away.

Two weeks to rebuild the mask, to silence the memories, to make sure Derrick Maddox showed up... and Dirty Divine stayed dead and buried.

And yet, as he lay down in the perfectly fluffed hotel bed, he couldn't ignore the truth pressing down on him.

The mask wasn't cracking.

It was splitting wide open.

Chapter 3
"Ghosts on the Pacific"

The plane cut through the clouds like a polished arrow, slicing its way westward across the vast expanse of the country. Derrick Maddox sat cocooned in first-class luxury, but his internal world was anything but serene. The engine hum, usually a calming white noise, felt like a drumbeat pressing into his skull. He adjusted the recline of his seat, shifting his long frame, but there was no finding comfort today—not when Los Angeles loomed on the horizon.

He stared blankly at the in-flight screen tracking their journey. A glowing line marked the path from New York to LA, the digital airplane inching closer to a place that held equal parts nostalgia and dread. Around him, the cabin bustled quietly—business travelers sipping scotch, influencers editing photos on tablets, a low murmur of conversation blending into the mechanical drone. Derrick tuned it all out, his jaw tense, fingers digging into the armrest.

Julian, seated next to him, tapped away on his laptop, blissfully unaware of the internal war raging beside him. Derrick closed his eyes, but it was a mistake. Images surfaced immediately—street names burned into memory, signs of long-gone clubs where Derrick once ruled the stage, the smell of beer and sweat, the flash of stage lights bouncing off disco balls.

A soft chime signaled the flight attendant approaching. "Can I get you anything, Mr. Maddox?"

Derrick blinked up at the young man with a practiced smile. "No, thank you," he replied, his voice calm, betraying none of the chaos within. The attendant retreated, and Derrick's façade cracked a little more.

The seatbelt light blinked off, and Julian leaned over. "ETA two hours. Wi-Fi's up if you want to scan the itinerary."

Derrick forced a nod and opened his tablet. The schedule appeared pristine and professional—two nights of keynotes, VIP meet-and-greets, a networking brunch, a podcast recording at a downtown studio, and a closing fireside chat. Derrick swallowed hard. Every bullet point brought a fresh wave of unease. Every line screamed *exposure, visibility, risk*.

He flicked away from the calendar and opened a private browser. His fingers hovered over the keyboard before finally typing in the names he hadn't searched in years: *Oil Can Oilers Los Angeles, Dirty Divine Drag Shows, Downtown Queer Archives*.

The Wi-Fi pinged alive with results, and Derrick's chest tightened. Some of the clubs were gone, bulldozed into parking lots or converted into trendy microbreweries. Others had survived, rebranded, still pulsing with neon promises. Old photos surfaced—grainy captures of half-drunken nights, posters with names he hadn't heard spoken aloud in decades.

His throat dried as he scrolled. There she was—Dirty Divine, immortalized in low-res chaos. A younger Derrick, hairier, wilder, coated in glitter and neon, middle finger proudly raised to the lens, mouth stretched wide in a shameless grin. The comments beneath the photos stung more than he cared to admit.

"*Divine was a hot mess and we LIVED for it.*"
"*Dirtiest mouth, loudest laugh, biggest heart.*"
"*Whatever happened to her? Disappeared after '07.*"

Derrick's chest ached. He closed the browser, but it was too late—the ghosts had been stirred.

As they descended into Los Angeles, the skyline crept into view through the airplane window. Derrick's stomach knotted. The downtown grid stretched beneath them like an old scar. He could see the areas he once haunted—Echo Park, Silver Lake, the forgotten pockets where queer life bloomed in all its raw, imperfect beauty. This wasn't just another city. It was a former life, reawakening.

The car ride to the hotel was a quiet one. Julian chatted about logistics, press, brand visibility, but Derrick only half-listened. The city flew past the tinted windows—storefronts replaced, clubs renamed, but enough remained that the memories gripped him like iron chains. Street corners where he'd shared late-night tacos with fellow queens. Alleys where he'd collapsed laughing after impromptu sidewalk performances. Bars where Dirty Divine had ruled the room with her vulgar jokes and unrepentant presence.

The hotel was sleek, towering, impersonal. Derrick stepped out of the car, cameras clicking as a small press group snapped promotional shots for the conference's media coverage. He forced his polished smile, stood tall, flexed the image of Derrick Maddox, Master of Masculine Empowerment. But inside, the crack deepened.

Julian whisked them through check-in and into the top-floor suite, a sprawling space with panoramic views of the city. Derrick didn't admire it. He shut the door, dropped his bags, and immediately retreated to the bedroom, pulling the curtains closed. He sat on the edge of the bed, head in his hands, lungs tight.

His phone buzzed. Julian's message blinked: *"Dinner reservation in 90 minutes. Let me know if you want to skip."*

Derrick set the phone aside and powered up his laptop. The compulsion to dig deeper took hold. He searched the names of old friends, fellow performers, those who had shared the tiny backstage spaces, the sticky floors, the inside jokes. Some profiles had gone dark—people vanished, moved on, disappeared. Others were still active, though quieter, settled into middle-aged obscurity.

Then there were the reminders of loss. Obituaries, memorial posts. Friends taken by addiction, by illness, by violence, by life's relentless cruelty. Names he hadn't spoken aloud in years now stared back from glowing screens. He wasn't just terrified of exposure—he was mourning.

Hours slipped by unnoticed. The sun dipped behind the buildings, and the suite grew darker. Derrick sat hunched over the laptop, scrolling until his eyes blurred, his heart heavy. This wasn't just a trip back to LA. It was an exhumation of a version of himself he had tried to forget but couldn't truly abandon.

A knock at the door pulled him back. Julian peeked in. "Pushed dinner back to room service. Thought you'd prefer privacy."

Derrick nodded silently.

Julian hesitated. "Everything alright?"

Derrick inhaled deeply, straightening his posture, pushing the Maddox persona back into place. "Fine. Just recalibrating. Long day."

Julian accepted it and retreated, leaving Derrick alone with the quiet hum of the city beyond the glass.

Later, Derrick stood by the window, the curtains half-open, watching the city lights blink to life. His reflection hovered ghost-like in the glass, older, stronger, more disciplined—but behind it lingered the shadow of Dirty Divine, grinning wickedly, whispering reminders of a life that refused to stay buried.

This trip was supposed to be a victory lap, a celebration of how far he'd come. But with every passing hour, Derrick realized it was shaping up to be a reckoning.

And he wasn't sure he was ready for it.

Chapter 4
"The Alpha Lie"

The recording studio was nothing like Derrick had expected. Tucked into the arts district of downtown LA, it was a refurbished loft space—open floor plan, exposed brick, dangling Edison bulbs—a hipster paradise that oozed with curated authenticity. Derrick sat in a minimalist leather chair, studio lights trained on him, headphones clamped over his ears, and a professional microphone extending from the desk like a serpent waiting to strike.

Across from him sat Blake Foster, the host of *Unfiltered Frequencies*, one of the most popular podcasts in the queer digital landscape. Blake was young, mid-twenties at most, hair bleached to platinum perfection, a piercing in one brow, dressed in a mesh top that revealed a wiry, tattooed frame beneath. Charismatic, quick-witted, and unapologetically flamboyant—Blake was every inch the new guard Derrick had worked so hard to differentiate himself from.

The producer counted them in through the glass window, and the signature jingle played, upbeat and rebellious.

"Welcome back to *Unfiltered Frequencies*, the show where queer voices don't hold back," Blake's voice boomed, energetic and effortlessly engaging. "Today, I'm joined by the man of the hour, Derrick Maddox—author, speaker, advocate for what he calls 'The Integrated Man.' Derrick, welcome to the show."

"Thanks for having me," Derrick replied smoothly, his tone calm, controlled, the practiced ease of public speaking rolling off his tongue.

"Let's get right into it," Blake grinned, fingers steepled under his chin. "You've become a lightning rod in the community. Some call you a breath of fresh air, others call you...well, the poster boy for internalized homophobia."

Derrick's jaw flexed slightly, but he smiled. "I think the value of discourse is that we don't all have to agree, Blake. My work focuses on allowing men—especially gay men—to reclaim parts of themselves they were told to hide or be ashamed of. Masculinity being one of them."

Blake leaned in. "Sure, but let's unpack that. Because in your latest book, you said—" Blake flipped to a page marked with neon tabs, "—'the modern gay man must reject performative queerness and instead cultivate dignified masculinity as a spiritual discipline.' Tell me how that doesn't sound like you're dragging—pun intended—an entire cultural expression under the bus."

The tension in the room sharpened. Derrick's shoulders remained square, his breathing even, but inside, something coiled. He gave a diplomatic smile. "It's about options. About telling men they don't have to adhere to one narrow lane. For decades, the most visible gay representation has been of high-energy, hyper-feminine personas, often in the form of drag performance. There's nothing inherently wrong with that, but it doesn't reflect the totality of our community. My work is about expanding the narrative."

Blake's grin didn't falter, but the eyes sharpened. "Expanding, or erasing? Because many feel your narrative throws a lot of shade on femmes and drag queens, and you can't exactly blame people for seeing a tone of judgment in your phrasing."

Derrick's fingers curled subtly on his lap, out of view of the cameras. A slow burn crept up his neck. "I'm inviting balance," he replied. "Balance that allows men who don't relate to those identities to feel validated too. Masculinity doesn't have to be toxic. It can be sacred."

Blake nodded slowly, eyes glinting. "Interesting. But the thing is, Derrick—you've become the 'anti-drag' guy. People quote you as saying drag reduces gay men to court jesters for straight amusement. That's strong language. Do you stand by that?"

The producer behind the glass was scribbling notes, the assistant watching wide-eyed. Derrick knew this was Blake's tactic—corner the guest, draw out raw reactions. He had prepared for this, had deflective answers in his back pocket, but now, sitting here, surrounded by unapologetic queerness, the questions bit deeper.

He inhaled deeply. "My criticism is about context," Derrick said, slower now. "Mainstream platforms have commodified drag, turning it into entertainment for straight audiences while ignoring the broader struggles of our community. That's what I critique—not the individuals, not the culture's roots."

Blake cocked his head. "But you've benefited from being the guy who says, 'Look at me, I'm not one of *them*. I'm a respectable masculine man.' You don't see a contradiction there?"

Derrick's throat tightened. The words came, smooth, rehearsed. "I've benefited from giving a voice to men who felt invisible within their own community."

Off-camera, his leg bounced. Under the table, his palm felt damp against the cool leather armrest. In his mind, flashes of nights twirling on sticky dance floors returned—Dirty Divine in her glory, cracking lewd jokes, commanding the stage, basking in joyous vulgarity. The contrast was stark, almost obscene.

Blake didn't relent. "So let me ask directly: have you ever done drag?"

The question hit like a slap. Derrick blinked, keeping his expression neutral through sheer willpower.

"Not in any way that aligns with my current values," Derrick replied carefully.

It wasn't a lie. It wasn't the whole truth either. A familiar twisting guilt settled in his gut.

Blake gave a knowing smirk, sensing the shift. "Fair enough. Let's pivot. You talk a lot about masculine energy and spiritual discipline—how do you define masculinity without making it prescriptive?"

Derrick latched onto the change in subject, guiding the conversation back into safer territory. For the remainder of the podcast, he delivered eloquent talking points about emotional resilience, mental fortitude, the importance of integrity over image. The room relaxed, but Derrick didn't.

After the recording wrapped, Blake shook his hand. The grip was firm, the smile polite but distant. "Thanks for coming on. The comments section is going to be a battlefield."

Derrick chuckled, masking the simmering unease. "I wouldn't have it any other way."

Back in the car, Julian was upbeat. "Handled that like a pro. This episode's going to chart high."

Derrick stared out the window as downtown LA zipped past, the skyscrapers and murals and neon remnants of his past. His reflection in the glass was sharp, commanding, flawless. Yet his mind replayed every pointed question, every moment of hesitation.

In his hotel suite, the walls seemed to close in. Derrick watched the interview go live within hours, clips already circulating on social media. Comments poured in—fans praising his composure, critics calling him a sellout, others questioning his authenticity.

He muted the notifications and stood before the full-length mirror. His posture was straight, his jawline firm, his suit impeccable. But inside, the lines were blurring. He heard Blake's voice echoing in his head, felt the weight of his own history pressing against the armor he'd so carefully built.

The lie wasn't in the words he'd spoken—it was in the parts he'd omitted. In the rejection of a former self who had once been free, unfiltered, messy but real.

As he peeled off his suit jacket and unbuttoned his shirt, Derrick caught a glimpse of his bare chest, the faint line of where old performance costumes used to squeeze him tight. He flexed his hands, knuckles tight, heart heavier than he'd allow anyone to know.

The crack was growing, widening with each breath. He wasn't sure how much longer the mask would hold.

Chapter 5
"The Oil Can Files"

Sleep eluded Derrick that night. Hours after the podcast recording, after room service had delivered an untouched dinner and Julian had retired to his own room, Derrick sat alone in the dim glow of his laptop screen. The city sprawled outside his window—Los Angeles humming with midnight life—but Derrick's world had shrunk down to a single point of focus: the search bar.

His fingers hovered above the keys, hesitation pulsing like a second heartbeat in his chest. He shouldn't do this. He knew that. Every instinct born of years of curated discipline screamed at him to shut the laptop, go to sleep, and prepare for tomorrow's keynote. But his fingers moved anyway, driven by a hunger he hadn't fed in years—a need to confront, to remember, to punish himself.

Oil Can Oilers Los Angeles, he typed, pressing enter before he could reconsider.

Google returned a flood of memories in pixels. Old flyers, grainy photos, forum posts on long-forgotten LGBTQ message boards. The years had not been kind to digital archives; some links were broken, some photos lost to time. But enough remained to pierce him straight through the armor he'd spent a decade constructing.

He clicked on a link that led to an archived Facebook album: *"Oil Can Oiler's Final Tour – 2007"*. The page loaded, and Derrick's breath caught.

There she was. Dirty Divine. In all her grotesque, glorious splendor.

The first photo showed Derrick—unrecognizable from his current polished self—grinning ear-to-ear with bright red lipstick smeared like war paint across his bearded face. His chest hair billowed from under a glittering halter top, balloon-stuffed breasts sagging comically to one side. His arms were wrapped around two fellow queens, all three of them doubled over with laughter, frozen in a moment of raw, unfiltered joy.

He clicked through more photos, each one a dagger. Derrick in mismatched thigh-high stockings, one slipping down his hairy calf; Derrick pouring cheap vodka down the gullet of a screaming audience member; Derrick standing triumphant atop a bar, bathed in neon light, leading a chant so vulgar the memory made his cheeks burn even now.

The comments beneath the photos hadn't aged a day.

"Best night of my life."

"God, Dirty Divine's roast of Trevor was legendary."

"Does anyone know where Dirty went after the final show? She just disappeared."

Derrick's throat tightened. He scrolled faster, clicking through albums, looking for... something. Proof of his evolution? Evidence that time had erased his past? But it was all still there. Archived by fans, preserved by friends, stamped into the digital universe with a permanence he could no longer control.

Panic prickled at the back of his neck. He slammed the laptop shut but the images remained behind his eyelids. He stood, pacing the length of his suite. His breathing was uneven, his thoughts racing through worst-case scenarios.

What if someone found these? What if Blake's producers dug deeper? What if those photos went viral, shared by the very community he claimed to represent? His mind painted the headlines: *"Derrick Maddox EXPOSED—The Bearded Queen Behind the 'Alpha Man' Movement."*

The mere thought made his stomach churn.

His phone vibrated. Julian.

"Reminder: Gym session at 7 AM, first meet-and-greet at noon."

Derrick tossed the phone onto the couch, running a hand through his short-cropped hair. He caught his reflection in the dark window—tall, broad, sharp-jawed, dressed in a fitted black T-shirt that emphasized his disciplined physique. A leader. An example.

Yet behind that reflection, just out of focus, he could almost see the ghost of Dirty Divine smirking back at him, one hand on her hip, the other flipping him off with glitter-painted nails.

He sat back down and reopened the laptop, fingers trembling. He dove deeper, pulling up old videos on YouTube, shaky cam footage of performances in tiny dive bars. There he was, leading a filthy parody of a pop anthem, voice cracking from cheap whiskey, joy radiating from every pore.

The crowd had adored him. He had adored them.

And then he had walked away. No goodbye, no farewell tour—just a sudden, clean break. He had burned Dirty Divine to the ground and risen from the ashes as Derrick Maddox, Gay Empowerment Coach, Spiritual Masculine Leader.

Was it all a lie?

No, Derrick told himself, pressing his palms against his eyes. It wasn't a lie. It was… transformation. Evolution. Growth.

But the fear wouldn't let go.

He typed in names—old colleagues, old queens, old friends. Some were still performing, some had vanished, a few had passed away. He found an Instagram account for *Miss Salty Taffy*, still performing camp drag in West Hollywood. Her bio read: *"Bearded, Loud, and Too Old for Your Bullshit."*

Derrick hovered over the follow button, but his hand froze. He closed the tab instead.

It was nearly four in the morning when Derrick finally collapsed into bed, exhaustion pulling him under. But his sleep was restless, broken by fragmented dreams of stage lights, smeared makeup, and crowds screaming his name—not *Derrick*, but *Divine*. He awoke tangled in sweat-damp sheets, the taste of cheap lipstick haunting his tongue.

The mask had cracked. And for the first time in years, Derrick wasn't sure he could keep it from shattering completely.

Chapter 6
"The First Dream"

Derrick's sleep was fractured from the moment his head hit the pillow. The comfort of high-thread-count sheets and temperature-controlled air couldn't calm the tempest within him. He drifted in and out of shallow dreams, each one a fragmented loop of memories refusing to stay buried. It wasn't until just past dawn that the dream took a sharper shape, pulling him under with a forceful grip.

In the dream, Derrick stood on a stage—but it wasn't the sleek, modern platforms he commanded today. This one was crooked, patched together with old plywood, glowing dimly under mismatched string lights. The air smelled of sweat, alcohol, and stale cigarette smoke. The audience was there, but faceless—shadows pressed against the walls, eyes like gleaming coals watching his every move.

He looked down at himself, and his breath caught. His body was a bizarre hybrid. From the neck down, he was Derrick Maddox: muscular arms, disciplined physique, designer loafers. But from the neck up, he was Dirty Divine in full, chaotic glory—eyeshadow smeared high on the brow bone, overlined red lips stretched into a cartoonish grin, a glittery beauty mark hovering above one cheekbone. His beard remained, exaggerated and teased out, woven with tinsel strands that caught the stage lights.

His heart pounded in his chest. He could hear it echo through the empty hollows of the dreamscape, louder than the distant hum of conversation from the faceless crowd.

Then came the music—an unholy mashup of motivational anthems and cheap bubblegum pop. Derrick knew the routine before the choreography kicked in. His body moved with instinctual muscle memory, launching into a campy dance number while his mouth belted out slurred, unapologetic lyrics dripping with sexual innuendo.

The crowd screamed in delight, hooting and howling, drinks sloshing in the air. He twisted, twirled, dropped to a deep squat, chest hair poking out from a crop top with rhinestones arranged to spell *DIRTY*. Every exaggerated shimmy, every vulgar grind brought louder cheers, but inside Derrick's dream-self was suffocating.

His voice cracked mid-song, and suddenly the background changed. The dive bar melted away into a massive conference stage. Sleek banners proclaimed *THE INTEGRATED MAN*, towering projection screens displayed his bestselling book cover. The faceless crowd remained, but the cheers turned to murmurs, then to jeers.

He stood center stage, still dressed in his bastardized hybrid ensemble, makeup running down his cheeks, fake breasts slipping sideways. He tried to speak—tried to explain, to rationalize—but no words came. Only the screech of a microphone feeding back against dead silence.

From the crowd emerged familiar faces: Blake from the podcast, eyebrows arched in smug satisfaction; Julian, jaw slack, betrayal written across his young features; stern-faced followers, loyal clients who once called him a mentor, their expressions now twisted with disgust.

A booming voice reverberated through the auditorium. *"Fraud."*

Another voice followed. *"Hypocrite."*

The chorus grew louder, pounding against his eardrums. *"Liar. Fake. Dirty Divine lives."*

Derrick's knees buckled. He reached for the microphone, but it dissolved in his hands. The stage beneath his feet began to crack, planks splitting and collapsing into darkness. The bright spotlight narrowed, suffocating him in its heat, the jeers turning to laughter—raucous, mocking, inescapable.

And through the shrieking din, Dirty Divine stepped forward, a mirror version of himself, cocking a heavily penciled eyebrow, lips curling into a predatory smile.

"You can't run from me, baby," she purred, voice dripping with unrepentant sass. *"I'm the best part of you. The free part."*

Derrick stumbled backward, but the stage gave way. He fell, tumbling through space, past images of both his lives—a young, drunken queen tipping back shots; a polished speaker signing books; a wild performer twirling on stage; a disciplined man meditating in a mountain retreat. Faster and faster, until the faces blurred, until the noise swallowed him whole.

His own scream pierced the dream, dragging him violently awake.

Derrick shot up in bed, sheets tangled around his legs, body slick with sweat. His heart pounded in his chest like a jackhammer, breath coming in short, ragged gasps. His hands trembled as they clutched the comforter, knuckles pale from the force of his grip.

A full-blown panic attack. The first in years.

It took him a full minute to register his surroundings—the luxury hotel suite, the faint buzz of Los Angeles beyond the insulated windows, the filtered morning light trying to push through the drawn curtains.

His chest burned as he forced himself to slow his breathing. Four counts in, hold, four counts out. He knew the drill, preached it himself in seminars. Yet it barely worked, the edges of his vision still narrowing, the suffocating weight of the dream pressing against his ribs.

A sharp knock sounded at the door. Julian's voice filtered through, laced with concern. "Boss? Everything good in there?"

Derrick scrambled from the bed, tugging on a hoodie to hide his sweat-soaked shirt. He wiped his face quickly with a towel from the bathroom, checking the mirror—red cheeks, wide, panicked eyes, damp hair matted to his forehead. He forced a grin, the kind that had built his career, and opened the door a crack.

Julian stood there, coffee in hand, brows knitted. "I thought I heard…" He trailed off, eyes scanning Derrick's disheveled appearance.

"Late-night cardio," Derrick lied, voice hoarse but attempting levity. "I couldn't sleep. Thought I'd knock out some extra steps around the room."

Julian didn't look convinced. "Your voice… you sound rough."

"Didn't hydrate enough," Derrick said, pushing the door open wider and ushering Julian inside. "Nothing a gallon of water and some green tea won't fix."

Julian set the coffee on the desk, watching Derrick move around the room, pulling back curtains, straightening the comforter, fussing over trivial details with forced energy.

"You sure?" Julian asked quietly.

Derrick paused, gripping the back of a chair until his knuckles whitened. The instinct was to lie, to brush it off, to lock the panic back behind a wall of discipline. He forced a grin instead, softer this time. "Just a rough night," he said. "No big deal. I'll muscle through it."

Julian gave him a hesitant nod, checking the time. "You have ninety minutes until the pre-event briefing."

"Plenty of time," Derrick replied, clapping his hands together with manufactured bravado. "Thanks for the coffee."

Julian left with one final look, the door clicking softly behind him.

Derrick leaned against the wall, sliding down until he sat on the floor, head resting back, eyes closing. His heart had steadied, but the unease lingered, coiled tight in his gut.

He told himself this was normal—nerves, stress, the price of success. But the truth rang louder than ever before.

The mask wasn't just cracking.

It was actively breaking apart. And Derrick Maddox, the master of control, was no longer sure he could hold it together.

Part II: Cracks in the Armor

Chapter 7
"Saboteur of Self"

The next few days in Los Angeles unfolded like a controlled implosion. On the surface, Derrick Maddox maintained his polished facade—smiles at photo ops, firm handshakes with event organizers, crisp delivery during his keynotes. But underneath, something corrosive gnawed at his composure, eating away at the foundation he had so carefully built over the past decade.

It began subtly. Small moments of irritation during sound checks, terse corrections to hotel staff over minor inconveniences. Julian noticed it first, flinching when Derrick's usually calm voice snapped at a junior event assistant for misplacing his protein shake. What would have once been a patient redirection now landed with a sharp edge.

"Do it right the first time," Derrick had muttered under his breath, jaw clenched tight, before storming off to his dressing room.

Julian chalked it up to fatigue—LA's schedule was grueling, after all—but by day three, there was no mistaking it. Derrick wasn't just tired. He was unraveling.

Interviews that had been secured weeks in advance were abruptly canceled. Derrick refused a scheduled podcast appearance, claiming "creative differences" with the host after reviewing their previous episodes. A live Q&A session, which typically ran an hour, was cut short after Derrick grew visibly annoyed with a question about inclusivity within the masculine identity movement.

Behind closed doors, Derrick paced endlessly, obsessively refreshing his phone. Notifications from social media piled up like an avalanche. For the first time in his career, Derrick didn't bask in the engagement—he feared it. Each ping carried the potential for discovery, for exposure.

His paranoia sharpened when he noticed a comment thread under one of his recent posts:

"Funny how these 'masc role models' always have a past. Anyone remember Dirty Divine? LA hasn't forgotten…"

It was like swallowing glass. Derrick's chest tightened, a cold sweat breaking across his skin. He clicked through the profiles but couldn't trace the origin. Burner accounts, vague usernames—cowards or saboteurs hiding in anonymity.

His mind raced. Who had started it? Someone from the old days? An envious rival? Blake Foster, smug from their recent podcast sparring match? Or was it just random internet noise feeding off his rising fame?

The more he thought about it, the worse it got.

Julian's gentle reminders were met with curt replies. "I said no interviews today," Derrick barked after Julian suggested a brief media appearance to mitigate the growing online speculation.

"But we need to get ahead of this," Julian pressed. "If you don't control the narrative, someone else will."

Derrick's stare was icy, his voice low and biting. "Control the team. Handle the schedule. I'll handle me."

Julian backed off, but worry lingered in his eyes.

That evening, during a rehearsal for his final LA keynote, Derrick's composure cracked fully. The AV technician missed a lighting cue—something minor, easily fixed—but Derrick exploded.

"This isn't amateur hour!" he shouted, startling everyone in the auditorium. "Do your damn job!"

Silence hung heavy. Julian stepped in, attempting damage control, while the technician, a young queer man barely in his twenties, shrank back in embarrassment. Derrick stormed off stage, heart hammering, temples pulsing.

In the privacy of his suite, he collapsed onto the couch, staring at the ceiling. The walls felt like they were closing in. He scrolled through social media, each comment a dagger:

"Derrick Maddox, the fragile alpha?"

"We see you, Dirty Divine."

"Nothing more dangerous than a man ashamed of himself."

His heart sank. He wasn't just battling internet trolls—he was battling himself. Every snide comment reflected back the truth he didn't want to face. His whole empire, his brand, his meticulously crafted identity—it was built on escape. On erasure. On running from a version of himself that had once been loud, wild, and free.

Was it guilt? Fear? Or both?

He no longer knew.

Late that night, after hours of spiraling, Derrick locked himself in the hotel gym. He pounded the treadmill, muscles burning, sweat pouring, as though he could outrun the truth. As though the rhythmic slap of his shoes on the belt could drown out the memories whispering in the back of his mind.

He stayed there until his legs gave out, collapsing onto the padded floor, chest heaving, vision blurry. The only thing louder than his ragged breath was the endless loop of doubts circling his brain.

Maybe someone was sabotaging him. Maybe there was a campaign to bring him down. Or maybe…

Maybe it was just him. Pulling the strings of his own demise.

The saboteur wasn't on Twitter. It wasn't some forgotten queen from the dive bars of LA.

It was the man in the mirror, fighting ghosts of his own making.

Chapter 8
"First Night Jitters"

The first night at the Downtown Marriott had all the makings of a grand spectacle. The ballroom had been transformed into a temple of modern masculinity—massive LED screens displayed Derrick's branding in sharp monochrome, the event logo etched into every surface from the podium to the water bottles. Rows of sleek black chairs stretched out under perfectly adjusted spotlights, ready to seat seven hundred eager attendees. Yet, as Derrick stood backstage, listening to the rising murmur of the crowd, his stomach felt like a knotted rope, tugging tighter with every passing second.

Julian buzzed around him like an efficient storm, adjusting Derrick's lapel mic, straightening his jacket, checking the run sheet. "Biggest crowd yet," he said, tone chipper, masking the nervous energy that hung thick in the air. "Live stream's up. Three thousand watching from home already."

Derrick's jaw tightened. "Good," he said, but it came out hollow.

This was supposed to be his victory lap. The culmination of years of work. A full house in Los Angeles—the city he had fled, the city he had risen above. Tonight was meant to be the definitive statement of his transformation. Yet all he could feel was the tremor in his hands and the unwelcome thump of his heart that refused to settle into its usual rhythm.

The emcee's voice boomed through the speakers, rattling the floor beneath his polished shoes. "Please welcome to the stage—the voice of a new era—Derrick Maddox!"

Applause roared as Derrick stepped into the blinding spotlight. The audience was a sea of expectant faces, a mix of sharply dressed professionals, fitness influencers, lifestyle coaches, and young men wide-eyed with hope. He'd seen this before—this hunger for guidance, for permission to exist without apology. Usually, it fueled him. Tonight, it felt like a burden too heavy to carry.

His rehearsed smile twitched as he took the microphone. "Good evening, gentlemen," he began, but there was a slight quiver in his tone that hadn't been there before. He swallowed it down and pressed on.

"Tonight, we talk about reclaiming what was stolen from us—our dignity, our strength, our right to define ourselves." The opening lines rolled off his tongue, but they felt detached, like he was listening to a recording of himself rather than speaking in real-time.

He moved through the first segment, laying out his Three Pillars, but the words lacked their usual gravity. The room, which should have been electric, felt oddly flat. He noticed it in the restless shuffle of feet, the sideways glances, the murmurs that broke the rhythm of his speech.

It was during the second segment—his segment on self-sovereignty—that it happened.

A voice from the back, loud enough to cut through the amplification, sharp enough to pierce the armor he wore like a second skin.

"Hey Derrick—what happened to Dirty Divine?"

Laughter rippled through the crowd, some shocked, some entertained, most curious. Derrick's heart seized in his chest. His tongue froze mid-sentence, his brain sputtering like an engine misfiring.

He blinked, scanned the crowd, but couldn't pinpoint the heckler. The lights blinded him, turning faces into blurry silhouettes. His throat went dry.

A crack formed in his composure. He stammered through the next sentence, words tangling awkwardly. "We... we are not defined by... by... our worst moments," he tried, but his voice lacked conviction.

Julian stood side-stage, eyes wide, mouthing *keep going*.

Derrick attempted to regain footing, pushing forward into the next section of his keynote, but the rhythm was gone. Where he normally wielded silence with precision, tonight, every pause felt like a gaping wound, every beat dragged longer than it should have. The audience shifted in their seats, uncomfortable, unsure.

A second heckle, lower but audible, "Funny how the alpha forgot his lines."

Heat surged up Derrick's neck, his pulse roaring in his ears. He rushed through the final minutes, skipping anecdotes, abbreviating points, collapsing a forty-minute speech into a fragmented thirty.

When the applause finally came, it was lukewarm, polite, obligatory. Derrick forced a smile, dipped his head, and walked off stage as quickly as decorum allowed.

Backstage was silent. Julian met him with a bottle of water, his usual praise replaced by a careful, "Rough crowd, but we'll course correct for tomorrow."

Derrick sat heavily on the dressing room couch, head in his hands. His phone buzzed relentlessly. Social media notifications piling in.

He clicked open the first clip. It was already circulating—a shaky live stream excerpt, captioned: *"Alpha Derrick Maddox SHOOK by heckler—can't even finish his speech!"*

Another clip followed, someone zooming in as Derrick's face visibly paled, the moment he froze immortalized in pixels.

Comments flooded in:

"Who is Dirty Divine??"

"This dude just glitched in front of a live audience lmao."

"You can take the queen out of the dive bar but…"

His stomach churned. He swiped through the avalanche of online feedback, each swipe another blow to the carefully constructed identity he'd spent years reinforcing.

Julian hovered. "We can scrub the tags, report the clips, mute the trolls. Focus on the morning session—redeem it."

Derrick nodded weakly, but the words bounced off the thick walls of rising panic.

He locked the door, leaned against the cool frame, and breathed in slow, shallow gasps.

This was supposed to be his conquest. Instead, night one had turned into his most public unraveling.

The ghosts weren't knocking anymore.

They were storming the gates.

Chapter 9
"The Mask Breaks"

The second night at the Downtown Marriott was meant to be redemption. It was Derrick Maddox's chance to reclaim control after a turbulent first evening. The production crew was on edge but efficient, Julian had tripled the run-throughs, and every piece of media was scrubbed clean. The energy buzzed with rehearsed perfection.

Yet as Derrick stood backstage, watching the countdown clock on the monitor tick toward zero, he felt a hollow chill in his chest where certainty used to live.

Julian appeared by his side, offering one last pep talk. "Keep it tight, stay on your core points, no detours tonight," he said quietly. "The crowd wants the leader, the powerhouse, not the apology."

Derrick nodded stiffly, adjusting his cuffs. His mouth said, "Understood." His gut said otherwise.

The roar of the crowd began to build as the house lights dimmed. He took his first step toward the curtain—then stopped.

Something snapped. Not a loud, cinematic crack, but a quiet inner snap, like a rope fraying beyond repair.

The mask was too heavy tonight. The curated lines, the stage-managed power poses, the sanitized version of himself—he couldn't stomach it for another hour.

"Julian," Derrick said, voice unsteady, "hold the opening. Ten minutes."

Julian blinked, confused. "That's not—"

"Ten minutes," Derrick repeated, stepping away from the stage, moving quickly toward the small green room tucked behind the curtain.

Inside, he stripped off the blazer and tie, yanking the mic off his lapel. His pulse raced, hands trembling as he moved to the mirror. The man staring back wasn't Derrick Maddox the icon—he was a man on the verge of implosion.

The image shifted in his mind. He didn't see the refined masculine leader anymore. He saw a ghost of himself—young, brash, covered in cheap glitter, howling with joy, daring the world to look away.

His breath grew ragged. The walls felt like they were closing in, the mask suffocating him, choking the last remnants of authenticity from his soul.

He moved to his garment bag, yanking it open, digging past the suits and sleek collared shirts until his hand landed on something buried at the very bottom: a zippered pouch of old performance wristbands and personal keepsakes Julian insisted on keeping "for good luck."

Fingers trembling, he pulled it open.

His hand closed around the familiar cheap fabric—fingerless neon gloves from his Oil Can Oilers days. They were tattered, but whole. Like him.

The world outside the green room buzzed with activity. Stage managers shouted cues, Julian paced nervously, and the crowd stirred in anticipation.

Derrick's heart steadied. His breath slowed.

No more pretending.

Five minutes later, when the emcee's booming voice welcomed Derrick Maddox back to the stage, there was a shift—a subtle murmur rolling through the crowd as Derrick appeared.

Gone was the suit. Gone was the alpha uniform.

Derrick walked out in black jeans, a simple tight t-shirt hugging his chest, neon gloves slipping over his hands. His beard remained sharp, his posture proud, but something else shone through—something raw, unfiltered, human.

For a moment, the room fell into a stunned silence.

Derrick took the microphone, no slides behind him, no cues in his ear.

"I had a speech prepared," he began, his voice steady but carrying a rasp of vulnerability, "but I think it's time you meet all of me."

The ripple in the audience deepened.

"I built this brand," he continued, "on discipline, strength, and honesty. But I left something out. I left someone out."

His thumb toyed with the edge of the neon glove.

"Before Derrick Maddox, there was someone called Dirty Divine. A loud, hairy, foul-mouthed queen who stomped on sticky bar floors and made people laugh until their sides hurt. And I buried her… because I thought success meant erasing my messiness, my joy, my history."

The crowd sat frozen.

"I told you to be your strongest self. Tonight, I realized that strength doesn't come from pretending to be untouchable. It comes from embracing all the parts of you—especially the parts you were taught to hate."

He paused, locking eyes with strangers who had come to see a polished guru but were meeting a man learning to forgive himself.

"I'm not here tonight to give you permission to be masculine. You already have that. I'm here to tell you… you don't have to amputate parts of yourself to be respected."

A few men in the crowd stood up, clapping slowly. More followed.

"Be the leader. Be the warrior. Be the outrageous queen. Be the gym rat, the theater kid, the entrepreneur, the glitter-clad dancer if that's who you are. Be everything."

The applause grew, swelling into something loud, raw, and real—no polite nodding, no calculated decorum. Real connection.

Derrick smiled—not the rehearsed grin but something softer, freer.

The mask broke… and underneath, Derrick Maddox stood taller than ever before.

Chapter 10
"Confrontation with Mirrors"

By the end of the week, the walls of the hotel suite had become a suffocating cage. Derrick Maddox stood in front of the floor-to-ceiling windows, arms crossed tightly against his chest, jaw clenched. The endless skyline of Los Angeles blinked back at him, the city that had shaped him, broken him, and now threatened to consume him again.

Julian stood nearby, shifting nervously from foot to foot. "You don't have to go down there," he offered quietly. "The schedule's clear. You've done enough. No one's expecting you to—"

"I'm going," Derrick cut him off, voice steely but strained. "I need to see it."

No further explanation was given. He traded his perfectly tailored suit for jeans, a black hoodie, and sunglasses. An effort to be invisible, though he knew better. There was no blending into the background in a place that remembered your name.

The ride-share driver didn't recognize him, or if they did, they didn't mention it. Derrick appreciated the silence. As they drove through the weaving arteries of the city, his chest tightened with every street sign that stirred dormant memories. Westlake, Echo Park, Silver Lake—all neighborhoods that had once been his stomping grounds, vibrant with life and chaos, now sterile through the car's tinted windows.

They passed the corner liquor store where he and the Oil Can Oilers had bought dollar tequila shots before shows. The graffiti-tagged alley where they prepped impromptu routines. The bodega where they'd scavenged greasy sandwiches after long nights drenched in sweat and cheap gin.

The car slowed as they entered the neighborhood where it had all begun. Derrick stepped out, instructing the driver to leave. He'd walk the rest of the way.

Time had not been kind to the old block. What was once a bustling strip of queer culture now looked sanitized, overtaken by corporate coffee shops and overpriced boutiques. The dive bar—*The Shack*—was gone, replaced by a minimalist juice bar advertising immunity shots and pressed greens.

Derrick's stomach lurched.

But a relic remained—down the side street, tucked between a vape shop and a vintage denim boutique, stood *The Ember*. He hadn't thought it would still be here. The sign was repainted, the entrance modernized, but it was the same building. The bones hadn't changed.

He walked toward it, heart rattling in his chest, and there, on the west-facing exterior wall, was the mural.

A kaleidoscope of colors stretched across the brick, a breathtaking homage to fallen queer activists, artists, performers. Portraits of legendary queens, poets, organizers, and misfits—all immortalized in vivid strokes. He swallowed hard, his throat tightening as his gaze landed on the familiar face of *Big Mama Roxie*, his first mentor, and further down, *Salty Taffy*, who'd taught him how to whip a wig into submission. Faces of his chosen family, gone too soon.

Then, toward the bottom corner, partially obscured by shadows, was a small, barely noticeable image—a cartoonish figure, wide grin, glittering eyes, balloon-stuffed chest bursting from a crooked corset.

Dirty Divine.

He took a step back, breath hitching. They hadn't erased him. They hadn't forgotten. They had honored him, in their way, as part of the tapestry of their shared rebellion.

Memories came crashing in like waves. The laughter, the freedom, the unapologetic embrace of chaos. Those nights hadn't been shameful—they'd been sacred. He hadn't been a joke—he had been alive, fully, vibrantly alive.

Tears burned at the corners of his eyes, blurring the mural. He wiped them away roughly, but the floodgates had opened.

He thought about what he'd built since then. The brand, the empire, the stoic image of Derrick Maddox: speaker, author, spiritual guide. All constructed on the bones of a man who had once danced barefoot on this very street, yelling obscenities into the night sky, finding strength in his outrageousness.

He thought about the people he'd left behind, the friendships that faded into dust, the mentors he never visited again, the promises he'd abandoned in his pursuit of 'respectability.'

The problem had never been Dirty Divine. It had never been the chaotic nights or the drunken chants or the bearded queens in duct-taped heels.

The problem was his denial of it. His rejection of the community that had nursed him into existence.

Derrick sat on the curb across from the mural, elbows resting on his knees, head bowed. For the first time in years, he allowed himself to grieve—not just for the friends lost, but for the pieces of himself he had buried beneath layers of designer fabrics and motivational slogans.

He sat there until the sun began to sink behind the skyline, casting long shadows across the mural, the colors deepening in the fading light.

When he finally stood, he felt lighter, steadier. The knots in his chest loosened just a little. The ghosts hadn't come to haunt him. They had come to remind him who he truly was.

The man in the mirror wasn't fractured because of his past. He was fractured because he had amputated a vital part of himself to fit into a box he thought would keep him safe.

And now, maybe, just maybe, it was time to reclaim all of it—the strength, the discipline, the humor, the flamboyance, the freedom.

Derrick took a final look at Dirty Divine's mischievous grin, a small smile tugging at his own lips.

"Thank you," he whispered, before turning back toward the city, a little less afraid of who he had been, and a little more certain of who he could still become.

Chapter 11
"Confession of the Cloth"

Derrick spent the next morning walking the streets of downtown Los Angeles, eyes open in a way they hadn't been in years. Every block seemed to whisper back to him. Not all memories were joyful—there were plenty of broken nights, but threaded between them were connections, community, a history that had been written in sweat and laughter and resilience.

At lunchtime, he found himself standing in front of *Casa Arco Iris*, the community center that had once been a safe haven during his early years. The building had been remodeled, fresh paint and updated signage replacing the rundown facade he remembered. Yet inside, the heart of the place remained unchanged.

Derrick hesitated before pushing through the glass doors. The air was cool, smelling faintly of incense and coffee. Posters lined the walls—support groups, activism workshops, mental health resources, drag shows, and queer youth outreach programs. It was alive with purpose.

At the reception desk sat a man with silver dreadlocks and glasses perched low on his nose. He looked up from his paperwork, his deep brown eyes widening in recognition.

"Well, well," the man said, standing slowly. His presence commanded the room, tall and broad, dressed in a flowing caftan patterned with vibrant geometric shapes. "If it isn't our prodigal son."

Derrick swallowed. "Father Troy."

Father Troy, ordained in a progressive queer-affirming church and a decades-long staple of the LA queer community, walked around the desk with deliberate steps. His lips curled into a smile, but his eyes remained guarded.

"What brings *Mr. Masculinity Manifesto* back to the old neighborhood?" Troy's voice was warm but laced with steel.

"I..." Derrick faltered, rubbing the back of his neck. "I just... needed to see the place. Needed to reconnect."

Troy gestured toward the small library space tucked into the corner. "Sit. Talk. I have the afternoon free."

Derrick followed, settling into a cushioned chair across from Troy, who poured them both cups of chamomile tea from a communal pot.

For a moment, they sat in silence.

Then Troy spoke, his tone even. "You've been making waves. Every feed I follow has your clips. Your books are on display at Barnes & Noble now. You've done well for yourself, Derrick."

Derrick offered a tight smile. "It's been a journey."

"Oh, I know," Troy nodded. "I watched it unfold. Watched you rise. Watched you distance yourself from the rest of us."

Derrick flinched. "It wasn't... I didn't mean to..."

Troy raised a hand. "Spare me the media spin. This isn't a podcast interview. You walked away from here and told the world you were 'redefining masculinity,' but all I heard was the sound of you shoving a wedge deeper into this community. Reinforcing that old lie—that some ways of being gay are respectable, and others are just... embarrassing."

Derrick's throat tightened. "That wasn't my intention."

"Intent doesn't erase impact," Troy replied calmly, but firmly. "Do you know how many young men sat in this room over the past few years, quoting you?

Saying they felt shame about enjoying a little flair, saying they felt weak if they didn't fit your ideal of 'disciplined masculinity'? You gave them language to hate themselves."

A wave of nausea rolled through Derrick's gut. He shook his head, defensively. "I was trying to balance the narrative. To show that we aren't limited to stereotypes."

"Balance isn't balance if it stomps on someone else's freedom," Troy countered. "You didn't *balance* anything, Derrick. You replaced one rigid box with another."

Derrick's defenses crumbled. He slumped forward, elbows on his knees, staring into his untouched tea. "I didn't know… I—maybe I got lost. Maybe I lost track of what I was doing."

Troy's voice softened slightly. "I believe you had good intentions. I know the boy who used to cry in the back room after gigs, wondering if there was more to life than the circus of survival. I know the kid who wanted to build something… but somewhere along the line, you stopped building bridges. You built a fortress instead."

The words hit harder than Derrick expected. He blinked back moisture threatening his vision.

"I felt like if I didn't become the exact opposite of Dirty Divine, I'd never be taken seriously," Derrick admitted, voice cracking. "I wanted to prove I was more than… that."

"But you *were* more than that," Troy said gently. "We all are. Complex. Multifaceted. You didn't have to erase Divine to be Maddox. You could've been both. You can still be both."

Derrick looked up, truly seeing Troy for the first time in years—not just as an elder or a guide, but as someone who had witnessed his entire evolution.

"Is it too late to fix this?" Derrick asked quietly.

Troy smiled, setting down his tea. "For who? For the internet? Maybe. They'll roast you no matter what you do. But for yourself? For the young people watching? For this community? No. Not too late. But you'll have to do more than just *say* the right words. You'll have to *live* them."

Derrick nodded slowly, his shoulders lowering, the burden loosening. "I'm tired of running, Troy."

"Then stop running," Troy said simply. "Start listening. Start showing up—not as a brand, but as a person. With flaws. With history. With stories that don't always make you look perfect."

For the first time in months, Derrick felt the knots in his chest ease. He wasn't sure what came next—if his career could survive this pivot, if his audience would embrace the whole of him—but for the first time, he realized that wasn't the point.

It wasn't about followers or sales or polished images.

It was about truth. And maybe redemption.

Troy rose, clapping a warm hand on Derrick's shoulder. "Welcome home, kid."

And for the first time in a long time, Derrick allowed himself to believe it.

Chapter 12
"Choosing the Stage"

The next morning, Derrick awoke earlier than usual, his body stirred not by obligation but by something deeper—a restless energy crackling beneath his skin. The sun peeked through the hotel curtains, casting golden beams across the carpeted floor. He stretched his limbs, each muscle sore from days of tension, but his mind felt clearer than it had in weeks. Last night's conversation with Troy played over in his head, not as an indictment, but as a lifeline.

Today would be different.

He sat by the window, sipping black coffee, staring out at the city that had once swallowed him whole and now felt like a place of reckoning. The weight on his chest remained, but it no longer felt suffocating—it felt purposeful.

The cursor blinked on his laptop screen, mocking him, but he didn't retreat. He opened a blank document and began to write.

This wasn't going to be the same keynote. There would be no hollow bravado, no polished platitudes. He would not hide behind the glossy façade of 'discipline' and 'strength.'

He wrote for two hours straight, fingers flying across the keys, pausing only to breathe through the flood of memories and realizations crashing against him. He rewrote the opening, reframed the pillars, dismantled the rigid walls he had so carefully constructed over the years.

His speech became a story—not a sermon, but a confession. The tale of a young man who had learned to perform, then learned to hide, and then convinced himself that hiding was healing. It was a story of self-deception, of internalized shame masquerading as discipline, of redemption not through reinvention, but through reclamation.

When he reached the closing lines, Derrick's chest heaved, a mix of catharsis and fear swirling within him. He re-read the speech aloud, voice cracking but steadying with each paragraph. This was the truth, raw and unvarnished.

Julian knocked lightly before entering, tablet in hand. "Morning check-in," he announced, but paused as he caught the shift in Derrick's demeanor.

"Cancel the morning run-through," Derrick said calmly. "I'm rewriting the keynote. Tonight, I'm doing it differently."

Julian blinked, caught off guard. "Are you sure? We're already fighting online narratives, and the organizers are expecting—"

"I know what they're expecting," Derrick cut in, but there was no anger in his tone, only quiet conviction. "But I won't repeat last night. I won't stand on that stage hiding behind half-truths. If I'm going to face that audience, it'll be as my whole self."

Julian hesitated, searching Derrick's face for traces of the storm that had consumed him earlier in the week, but instead found clarity. He nodded slowly. "Alright. What do you need?"

"Time," Derrick said. "And trust."

"You have both," Julian replied simply.

For the rest of the afternoon, Derrick remained in his suite, reviewing the rewritten keynote, fine-tuning the flow, removing rehearsed lines that no longer resonated. He replaced them with honesty, vulnerability, and complexity. He dug into old archives, finding photos of himself during the Dirty Divine years, embedding one into his opening slides—an unapologetic embrace of the very history he had fled.

When the time came to dress, he chose differently. No dark, somber suits. Instead, he donned a sharp ensemble accented with color—a subtle nod to his past flamboyance without compromising his present identity. A deep plum jacket, crisp white shirt, no tie, sleeves rolled up to reveal inked reminders of journeys traveled and lessons learned.

Backstage, Julian and the rest of the team looked on, wary but intrigued. The room buzzed with anticipation, the atmosphere charged with curiosity about what Derrick would deliver.

"I'm not giving you the old Maddox tonight," Derrick said to his crew, looking each in the eye. "I'm giving you the man behind him."

The emcee's voice echoed through the grand ballroom, calling Derrick to the stage. He exhaled deeply, shoulders squaring, pulse steady, and walked out under the lights.

This time, when Derrick stood at the podium, there was no barrier between him and the crowd. No carefully manufactured distance. Only a man, standing whole, in front of an audience expecting answers and witnessing authenticity.

He looked out at the sea of faces and, instead of fear, felt a strange calm settle over him.

"Good evening," he began, voice strong but warm. "Tonight, I want to tell you a story—not just about discipline or strength, but about truth. About the masks we wear, the identities we shed, and the liberation in accepting every version of ourselves."

And as he launched into his story, Derrick felt something shift—not just in the room, but within himself.

He had chosen his stage, and this time, he stood on it as a man fully seen.

Part III: The Integrated Self

Chapter 13
"The Reclamation of Masculinity"

The ballroom hummed with muted conversation as Derrick waited behind the curtain, the seconds ticking down to his final keynote in Los Angeles. But this wasn't the same Derrick Maddox who had stumbled through his first night here—trapped in panic, haunted by shame, hiding behind perfected lines.

This was a man on the cusp of reclamation.

Julian stood by his side, unusually quiet, tablet in hand. "Crowd's bigger tonight," he murmured. "Even some press slipped in." He hesitated, then added, "This version of the keynote… it's raw, Derrick. Are you sure you're ready for this?"

Derrick didn't answer right away. He closed his eyes, feeling the familiar thrum of adrenaline. But this time, there was no cold dread, only a steady rhythm. "I'm not here to be safe," he said quietly. "I'm here to be real."

Julian gave a tight nod. "Then let's give them the real."

The music cue hit. The emcee's voice rang out.

And Derrick walked into the light.

But tonight, he didn't go to the podium.

Instead, he stepped down from the stage and walked directly into the crowd, microphone in hand. Gasps rippled through the audience as they turned in their seats to follow his movement.

"I've stood on this stage all week, preaching strength, discipline, and control," Derrick began, his voice amplified yet intimate. "But I've realized something dangerous happens when strength turns into self-denial—when discipline becomes a disguise."

He kept moving, stopping near the back, locking eyes with strangers who had only ever known him through curated soundbites.

"I've spent years building a fortress around myself—pretending that if I could master my body, my mind, my image, I could outrun my history."

A hush fell over the ballroom.

"Some of you came here expecting the Maddox you've seen online," Derrick continued, "the version that fits a brand of masculinity scrubbed clean of flamboyance, of chaos, of imperfection. But I've spent the last week realizing the cost of that performance."

He walked back toward the stage, stepping up, planting himself center stage under the full glare of the lights.

"And I've decided I'm done being a performance."

The screen behind him lit up with a stark, unedited image: Derrick Maddox in his Dirty Divine days—grinning wide, chest hair glistening beneath neon lights, makeup smeared but joyful.

A collective murmur swept through the crowd.

"For those of you who don't know, this was me," Derrick said, pointing to the screen. "This is also me. And the man you see standing here tonight? He's both. He's every laugh, every stumble, every reinvention, every contradiction."

Derrick's voice grew steadier, conviction rising like a tide.

"Tonight isn't about discarding masculinity. It's about expanding it. About creating space for discipline and delight. For stoicism and sass. For leadership and lightness. For strength that doesn't come at the cost of your soul."

The lights softened as the screen filled with images—not just of Derrick, but of queer men in every shade of masculinity: fathers cradling their children, drag performers in full glory, athletes, artists, activists, men laughing, crying, living without apology.

"We don't have to choose between power and playfulness," Derrick said. "Between respect and joy. Between being taken seriously and being our fullest, weirdest, most alive selves."

Applause started small, then swelled—spreading like wildfire across the room.

Derrick's chest loosened. His smile was finally unforced.

"This is the reclamation," he said, his final words clear and unapologetic. "Not of some polished ideal—but of our messy, magnificent, integrated selves."

The ovation erupted. Derrick didn't flinch or downplay it. He stood tall, arms open, fully visible.

And for the first time, he didn't feel like he was conquering the room.

He felt like he had come home to himself.

#

The applause still echoed in his ears as he returned to his suite that night, but so did the aftershock.

Social media lit up within minutes. Clips flooded every platform—#NewMasculinity trended by midnight. Videos spliced his speech with audience reactions. Younger queer audiences swarmed the content, commenting with: *"Finally, someone gets it."* and *"This is the evolution we needed."*

But backlash struck too.

Traditionalists from Derrick's prior base bristled at his pivot. Comments accused him of selling out, of pandering, of abandoning the 'real men' movement. Influencers who had once quoted him now posted critiques: *"Confused." "Weak." "Just another performer in disguise."*

Derrick read every word. The praise warmed him. The criticism stung.

But for the first time, it didn't control him.

Later that night, he turned on his phone's front camera. No filters. No lighting tricks. Just Derrick, seated on his hotel bed, speaking plainly to whoever still listened.

"Critique me. Challenge me. But understand this— the only person I'll ever betray again is the one I used to be when I was afraid to show up whole."

His voice didn't tremble. It resonated.

His following dipped and surged wildly over the next few days. But those who stayed—those who embraced the message—were fiercer, more engaged, more human.

And for Derrick Maddox, this wasn't a rebrand.

It was the beginning of his truest chapter yet.

Chapter 14
"Backlash and Breakthrough"

The morning after Derrick's landmark keynote, the world felt louder. Alerts pinged off his phone in a never-ending stream—mentions, tags, news headlines, debate threads, and commentary videos. Every platform was ablaze with opinions about Derrick Maddox and his raw declaration of a "New Masculinity."

He sat at the breakfast table in his hotel suite, refreshing social feeds between sips of lukewarm coffee. Julian sat across from him, tablet in hand, rifling through the torrent of data.

"Well," Julian said, tapping on the screen, "you've made yourself impossible to ignore."

Derrick arched an eyebrow. "Let's hear it."

Julian scrolled. "CNN picked it up, running a 'Changing Faces of Masculinity' segment. Vice wrote a glowing op-ed—'The Bearded Queen Who Dismantled the Alpha Fantasy.' BuzzFeed clipped your Dirty Divine moment and captioned it 'Queer Joy Meets Leadership Goals.' You're trending globally."

Derrick took another slow sip of coffee. "And the other side?"

Julian sighed. "Fox News ran a hit piece within hours: 'Alpha Leader Goes Soft, Betrays Movement.' Some of your old conservative backers—Strength Brotherhood, Apex Elite Circle—issued statements cutting ties. They're calling you the latest victim of 'rainbow corruption.'"

Derrick nodded, unsurprised. "Let them."

But the backlash wasn't limited to just talking heads. His inbox was flooded with disgruntled followers, messages ranging from disappointment to outright vitriol. Former collaborators posted reaction videos, denouncing his pivot. Hashtags like #FakeAlpha and #MaddoxMeltdown trended alongside #NewMasculinity.

Yet, on TikTok and Instagram, a different wave was rising. Young queer men stitched his clips with their own testimonies, talking about freedom, about complexity, about permission to be whole. Genderqueer voices echoed his speech, saying it resonated beyond binary norms. Fitness influencers celebrated a message that balanced strength with softness. The phrase "Authentic Masculinity" spread like wildfire.

Derrick watched the cultural storm brew with a strange sense of calm. For every angry denouncement, there was a heartfelt message of gratitude. For every unfollow, there were two new connections made with people who saw him fully.

Media invites flooded in—debates, TV panels, podcast interviews. His publicist tried to triage the demand, but Derrick declined most of them. He didn't want to be a spectacle or a soundbite. He didn't want to defend himself to audiences invested in misunderstanding him.

Instead, he chose select platforms—long-form interviews where nuance could breathe, where conversation could go beyond sensational headlines.

His first major appearance was on *The Human Project Podcast*, known for thoughtful discourse. Seated in a minimalist studio, Derrick laid out his journey—his past as Dirty Divine, his transformation, his shame, and his rediscovery of joy.

"It's easy to get addicted to applause," Derrick confessed. "But it's even easier to get trapped by the approval you fear losing."

The episode went viral. Not for scandal, but for sincerity.

The weeks that followed were chaotic but clarifying. Derrick lost sponsors, but gained unexpected allies—mental health advocates, queer youth leaders, feminist circles who found his narrative refreshing.

Online debates raged: *Was Derrick Maddox brave or hypocritical? A visionary or a sellout?*

Within queer spaces, conversations deepened. Panels formed around rethinking masculinity—not just for gay men, but for the entire LGBTQIA+ spectrum. Derrick's name came up in college classes, in activist workshops, in casual conversations between lovers and friends.

Julian, monitoring the shifting tide, smiled over their shared dinners. "You didn't just break the internet, you cracked open a discussion people were too afraid to have."

Derrick, weary but content, shrugged. "It was overdue."

The backlash persisted. Trolls remained. Critics doubled down.

But Derrick stood firmer than ever, grounded not in an image, but in himself.

As the world debated, dissected, and argued, Derrick quietly built something new—not a brand, but a legacy. One that made room for softness and strength, discipline and playfulness, structure and chaos.

One that allowed every boy, man, and nonbinary soul to embrace their own version of power.

And in that storm of backlash, Derrick found his breakthrough.

Chapter 15
"Quiet Aftershock"

In the weeks following his cultural firestorm, Derrick Maddox stepped away from the whirlwind. He didn't vanish, but he intentionally receded from the public's glare, pausing appearances, scaling back social media, and declining most interviews. The world spun feverishly without him, arguments flaring and cooling, but for Derrick, it was time to tend to something far more important—his own neglected self.

It started with therapy. Not the performance-driven, optimization-style counseling he'd leaned into in past years, but real, gut-level therapy with an older queer therapist named Rafael who wore colorful cardigans and didn't let Derrick hide behind polished narratives. Their sessions were messy, filled with awkward silences, reluctant admissions, and more than a few sessions where Derrick left emotionally raw but lighter.

Rafael challenged him. "You didn't just erase Dirty Divine—you erased joy. You buried it under productivity and image management."

Derrick wrestled with that, week after week, learning to untangle the warped threads of ambition and fear that had defined him for so long.

Yoga became part of his routine, more for the quiet than the stretches. He showed up to early morning classes in Echo Park, slipping into anonymity among retirees, college students, and flexible bodies unconcerned with his past notoriety. On the mat, he confronted stillness, breathwork, the rebellion of doing something with no outcome other than presence.

He reached out to old friends—the few who were still around, who hadn't been lost to time, distance, or his self-imposed exile. Reconnecting wasn't always easy. Some met him with warmth, others with justified caution, some with bitter honesty about how his rise had left them behind. Derrick didn't offer excuses. He listened. Apologized where necessary. Repaired where possible.

One evening, he visited Father Troy again. They sat in the courtyard of Casa Arco Iris, sharing horchata and watching the youth program rehearse a dance routine. Troy grinned. "This is your real legacy—not viral clips. These kids, these spaces, this community."

Derrick smiled, a quiet, genuine smile. "I'm just learning to show up better."

His days became simple—therapy, movement, meals with old friends, long walks through neighborhoods filled with old memories. Some mornings, he volunteered at local shelters, anonymously folding clothes and organizing donations, no social media posts, no cameras, no agenda beyond human connection.

And yet, despite the quiet, the world hadn't forgotten him. The debate raged on in online spaces. Derrick's name surfaced in symposium panels, think pieces dissecting his message, podcasts exploring the intersections of masculinity and queerness. Some remained critical, others celebratory, but Derrick no longer checked the feeds obsessively. Julian kept an eye on things, occasionally forwarding messages of impact from young people who felt seen for the first time.

On one of their walks, Julian asked, "Do you miss it? The stage, the spotlight?"

Derrick thought for a long moment. "I miss connection," he admitted, "but not the performance."

He found himself questioning his place within the very movement he'd helped ignite. Was he a leader? A cautionary tale? A bridge between old paradigms and emerging identities? Or just a man finally learning how to live without apology?

The answer didn't come easily. Some days, Derrick felt at peace, other days he felt adrift, but for the first time, he embraced the uncertainty. Not every journey required a map. Some only required honesty and the willingness to stay present.

His brand settled into something more organic. Fewer staged photos, more thoughtful writing. He restructured his speaking engagements to include storytelling and conversation, not just motivation. He collaborated with queer wellness groups, mental health organizations, and youth programs.

Months later, Derrick sat at a small café, journaling by hand. Across from him, a young nonbinary person approached hesitantly. "You're Derrick Maddox, right? I just wanted to say… your speech changed how I see myself. I never thought I could be strong and soft. It helped."

Derrick's heart warmed. "Thank you," he said simply.

In that moment, he realized his place wasn't fixed to stages or labels. It was fluid, evolving, messy, and beautiful.

In the quiet aftershock, Derrick found freedom—not in controlling the narrative, but in living truthfully within it.

Chapter 16
"Letters from the Past"

The shift in Derrick Maddox's life grew more profound with each quiet day, but nothing jolted him more than the messages that began arriving, first in trickles, then in waves.

It started with an email titled *"From One Oiler to Another."* The name in the sender field made Derrick's chest tighten—Casey, known back then as *Cherry Bombshell*, one of the sharpest tongues and brightest hearts in the Oil Can Oilers troupe.

The email was blunt.

"Wasn't sure I'd ever write this. I swore you disappeared on us and sold out. But that speech... you sounded like someone I used to know. Don't know if I forgive you yet. But maybe I don't hate you anymore. Cherry."

Derrick sat frozen for a full ten minutes after reading it, unsure whether to laugh, cry, or reply.

Within days, more messages poured in. Instagram DMs, Facebook friend requests, emails from accounts long forgotten. Some were short and acidic:

"Nice to see you remember where you came from. Took you long enough."

Others were warm, filled with nostalgia and tentative kindness:

"Divine was the fiercest. Glad to see Derrick finally let her out for some air."

A few cut deep:

"I cheered for you once. Then you made me feel like a punchline. Took me years to love my queerness again."

Derrick read every message, no matter how painful. He made no attempt to curate the experience, no filtering of the feedback. This was the reckoning he owed.

Some he responded to immediately, others he let simmer, choosing to write from a place of sincerity rather than defensiveness. He wrote private apologies, paragraphs of honest reflection, admitting his failures without cloaking them in justification.

To those he had left behind without a word, he explained the fears that had driven him, not as an excuse but as context. To those who felt erased by his hypermasculine narrative, he acknowledged the harm and expressed his commitment to doing better.

One evening, he sat down with Julian, scrolling through the open messages. "I thought burying Divine was power," Derrick admitted quietly. "Turns out my real power is owning every piece of my story."

Julian nodded. "It's never too late to repair." Then, with a wry smile, "You should host a reunion. Bring the Oilers together. See who's still willing to share a stage."

The idea felt both terrifying and exhilarating.

The next morning, Derrick posted publicly, writing a long-form letter addressed to his past—*To the Ones I Left Behind.* It wasn't polished brand content, but raw emotion.

In it, he apologized to former friends and mentors, acknowledged the damage of his silence, and invited dialogue. He didn't ask for immediate forgiveness. He asked for honesty, for conversation, for a chance to show up as the whole version of himself.

The response was overwhelming. The post circulated across queer circles, shared by drag queens, activists, youth workers, and everyday people who had witnessed both Derrick's rise and his fall.

Some declined his olive branch, politely or not.

But many accepted.

Invitations to small meetups flowed in. Drag performers tagged him in throwback photos. Activists messaged about collaborations. Even grumpy Cherry Bombshell agreed to a phone call, and three hours later, they were swapping scandalous old stories and tentative plans for the future.

Derrick's calendar filled, but this time not with high-profile panels or corporate bookings. It filled with coffees, dinners, quiet reunions, and community forums. Spaces where the stage was even, where the exchange was mutual.

Every conversation peeled back layers he hadn't realized he still carried. Guilt. Ego. Longing. But beneath it all, a growing sense of belonging—the kind he hadn't felt since those wild nights in the Oilers crew.

In those letters and reconnections, Derrick found clarity: his power wasn't in leading from above, but in walking alongside. His platform wasn't a pulpit, but a gathering place.

The journey wasn't about redemption for fame's sake. It was about wholeness, community, and honoring every version of himself—bearded diva, disciplined speaker, messy human.

And for the first time in a long time, Derrick Maddox didn't just feel free.

He felt home.

Chapter 17
"The New Sermon"

Six months later, the world Derrick Maddox inhabited felt different—not because it had shifted, but because he had. He moved through it with less armor and more openness, no longer consumed by image maintenance or fear of exposure. The world still debated his message, his transformation, his contradictions, but Derrick had made peace with it.

Standing backstage at the grand opening of *The Grove*, Derrick felt a sense of nervous excitement he hadn't experienced in years. *The Grove* was his newest project—a retreat center nestled in the hills just outside Los Angeles. What had once been a dilapidated ranch had been transformed into a vibrant queer haven, blending spiritual wellness, masculine embodiment, and unapologetic camp celebration.

The design reflected the integration Derrick had fought for: meditation gardens and yoga domes stood beside drag cabaret stages; strength-training gyms neighbored art studios filled with glitter, paints, and costume racks. There was a fire circle for raw storytelling nights and a river deck for moments of quiet reflection. It wasn't about curating the queer experience into one aesthetic—it was about honoring its spectrum in full color.

Derrick looked down at his hands, lightly dusted with gold shimmer—a nod to Dirty Divine, who was no longer buried, but embraced. His attire blended elements of his past and present: tailored slacks with a velvet vest, his chest hair peeking through a loose button-down, sleeves rolled up, a simple beaded bracelet gifted by Father Troy resting on his wrist.

Julian approached, clipboard in hand but grin wide. "You ready?"

Derrick exhaled. "Ready. Nervous, but ready."

Julian clapped his shoulder. "First of many. You're opening something people didn't know they needed."

The opening ceremony was simple. No corporate sponsors, no camera crews, no grand media spectacle. Just community—people from all walks of life gathered under the grove's largest oak tree, seated on picnic blankets and benches. Old friends from his Oiler days, new faces from queer youth shelters, community elders, spiritual leaders, activists, and even a few fitness enthusiasts who had found Derrick's evolution resonant.

Derrick stepped up to the makeshift wooden stage, microphone in hand, heart steady but full.

"Thank you for coming," he began, voice carrying softly across the quiet clearing. "Thank you for being part of something I thought I'd never have the courage to build."

He spoke of *The Grove*, not as a brand, but as a sanctuary. A space where queer souls could reconnect with themselves beyond society's expectations. A space where strength didn't require suppression, where vulnerability wasn't weakness, where flamboyance wasn't derided, and discipline wasn't distorted.

Then, as the evening settled into golden hour, Derrick delivered his new sermon—the foundation for his next speaking tour titled *The Integrated Man*.

"For too long, we've been told we must choose—choose between softness and strength, between joy and respect, between spirituality and sexuality," Derrick said. "But these are false choices. The integrated man, the integrated soul, rejects those binary prisons. He does not shrink to fit into someone else's comfort zone. He expands to embrace all of himself."

He spoke of a masculinity rooted not in dominance but in stewardship; a selfhood that honored both discipline and play. He quoted lessons from Father Troy, from old Oiler memories, from yoga sessions and therapy breakthroughs.

"The goal," Derrick said, "isn't to be alpha or beta, tough or tender. The goal is to be whole. To show up as all of who we are, without apology. To laugh from the gut, to cry without shame, to lead without crushing others, to love without condition."

The crowd listened, enraptured. Many filmed on their phones, some wiped away quiet tears, others simply closed their eyes and let the words settle into their bones.

As Derrick concluded, his final words resonated through the grove:

"Your strength is not diminished by your joy. Your discipline is not undone by your softness. Your masculinity is not defined by rejection—it is defined by integration. Welcome home."

The applause was thunderous, not forced or performative, but raw and real. Derrick's chest swelled, not with ego, but with belonging.

The retreat opening marked the start of a new chapter. Over the next months, Derrick traveled less for corporate speaking and more for community gatherings, wellness summits, and educational forums. *The Integrated Man* tour visited college campuses, queer community centers, spiritual retreats, and even correctional facilities.

His message reached unexpected audiences— young queer men finding peace with their identity, older gay men reconnecting with lost joy, transmasculine individuals finding space within the discourse, straight allies learning to embrace nuanced masculinity.

Criticism persisted, but Derrick no longer sought universal approval. He wasn't selling a product—he was sharing a life lived fully.

One evening, after hosting a fireside reflection at *The Grove*, Derrick sat beneath the stars, sipping tea. Julian joined him, grinning. "You know," Julian mused, "if someone had told me years ago that Derrick Maddox would be leading glitter-covered meditation circles, I would've laughed."

Derrick chuckled. "So would I. And I would've been wrong."

As laughter mingled with the crackling fire, Derrick finally understood what it meant to be at peace—not the peace of silence, but the peace of truth, of wholeness.

His journey wasn't about escaping Dirty Divine or conforming to Derrick Maddox. It was about being fully, gloriously both.

And from this integrated space, he would teach others—not from a stage above, but from the circle within.

The final scene of Derrick's new chapter wasn't the applause or the headlines—it was the quiet, consistent heartbeat of community, of radical self-love, of chosen family.

And with each heartbeat, Derrick lived fully, for himself, for those he had loved, and for those still learning to love themselves.

Epilogue

Years passed, but the quiet revolution Derrick Maddox ignited didn't fade. Instead, it grew, branching out like the mighty oaks at The Grove, touching corners of the world Derrick had never thought possible.

From his spot on the hillside deck of The Grove, Derrick watched as groups of young men, nonbinary folks, and even older queer men gathered in circles below. Some wore suits, others shimmering makeup. Some flexed muscles honed in gyms, others swayed to internal rhythms, free of the chains of presentation expectations. Derrick smiled, watching them laugh together, meditate together, lift weights, dance, and cry openly in fireside confessionals.

It was a Saturday afternoon in early summer, and the latest cohort of *The Integrated Man* retreat was in full swing. Derrick could hear the echoes of conversation from the nearby yoga dome, snippets of laughter from the river deck, and the distant beat of bass-heavy dance remixes coming from the cabaret lounge where a newly formed camp drag troupe practiced their routines.

Julian approached, bringing fresh tea. His graying hair betrayed the years, but his energy remained youthful. He sat beside Derrick, nudging his shoulder gently. "You seeing what I'm seeing?"

Derrick nodded slowly, his heart full. "A future that doesn't need to choose between power and joy."

It hadn't been an easy journey. The old guard never fully forgave him. Some corporate speaking circuits remained closed, his name blacklisted by those who clung to rigid definitions of masculinity. But in exchange, Derrick found something far more sustaining: authenticity, belonging, and a living legacy of people embracing their whole selves.

The letters still came, sometimes handwritten, sometimes via social media, sometimes whispered in person at quiet moments of connection. Stories from men who had finally embraced their softness, from trans men who found comfort in The Grove's nuanced spaces, from femme-presenting men who reclaimed joy without shame, and from allies who dismantled their own internalized stereotypes.

Every year, new facilitators joined the ranks at The Grove, blending disciplines—therapists, drag queens, bodybuilders, yogis, writers—all co-creating a space that celebrated the vast, vibrant spectrum of masculinity and queerness.

Derrick remained a guiding presence, but no longer the sole face of the movement. He had made a point to decentralize leadership, encouraging younger voices to rise, allowing the mission to evolve beyond him.

Watching from his quiet perch, he reflected on his own transformation. From Dirty Divine's chaotic glamour to Derrick Maddox's stern discipline, and now, something freer—a man no longer running from his contradictions but living through them.

He thought of Father Troy, now retired but occasionally visiting to deliver soulful workshops. He thought of the Oil Can Oilers, some lost to time, others who returned for anniversary celebrations, their laughter filling The Grove like an old favorite song. He thought of the hard days—of panic attacks, criticism, public humiliation—but now they felt distant, almost like faded scars that no longer ached.

As the evening approached, Derrick made his way down the hill to the main circle, where tonight's closing ceremony would be held. Participants were gathering, laying down blankets, preparing to share stories and intentions before the crackling bonfire.

Before stepping into the circle, Derrick paused, taking in the full sight: people unapologetically present, masculinity stretched beyond old definitions, freedom stitched into every laugh, every glittered cheekbone, every embrace between brothers who had learned to soften.

And he smiled—a wide, genuine, unburdened smile—because he knew, finally and completely, that his greatest impact had come after his greatest fear. Not in the curated perfection of his former persona, but in the messy, glorious, whole-hearted embrace of every shade of himself.

As the first stars appeared in the indigo sky, Derrick took his seat in the circle, not as a leader above, but as a member within, heart steady, spirit free.

And the circle began to hum with life, carrying forward a legacy not built on image, but on truth, connection, and the radical power of integration.

About the Authors

Alan Bourgeois began his writing career at the age of 12, writing screenplays for the Adam-12 show. Despite not submitting them for review, this experience sparked his passion for writing. However, he followed the advice of his generation and pursued higher education to secure a stable job. It wasn't until 1989, after taking a writing class at a community college, that Bourgeois wrote a short story that was published. Since then, he has written over 48 short stories and published more than 10 books, including the award-winning spiritual thriller "Extinguishing the Light."

Bourgeois has become a champion for authors and founded the Texas Authors Association in 2011 to help Texas authors better market and sell their books. This led to the creation of the Texas Authors Museum & Institute of History, Inc., and the first online museum of its kind, the Texas Authors Museum. He also created several short story contests and fundraising programs for Texas students and consolidated small-town book festivals into the Lone Star Festival, promoting Texas authors, musicians, artists, and filmmakers. In 2016, he founded the Authors Marketing Event and added a Certification program in 2017, allowing attendees to gain accreditation for their hard work in learning book marketing. His recent focus has been on assisting authors of all levels to become successful Authorpreneurs through the Authors School of Business, which offers programs to help grow their careers. He is currently working with NFTs for authors to help them increase their income channels.

Other Books by the Author

Bourgeois has over 45 books published. What follows are just a collection of books published in the last five years.

Voices of Stillness & Fire
Where hope meets resistance, ordinary people kindle extraordinary change.

From a bluebonnet-strewn Texas dream to a covert tunnel network battling a modern-day purge, these twelve powerful stories trace a single arc: when we dare to feel with one another, we ignite the strength to remake the world. Meet writers rediscovering their legacy, lovers crafting magic in wax and gold, leather-clad elders proving age is power, professors and pastors unlearning dogma, and underground rebels turning grief into action. Every page brims with radical empathy, queer joy, and the unbreakable resolve of those who refuse to be erased. Whether you crave heart-warming inspiration or pulse-pounding dystopian suspense, *Voices of Stillness & Fire* will leave you burning to stand up, reach out, and write the next chapter of hope yourself.

The Shadow Directive: The LGTBQIA+ Community will Not be Erased
The Shadow Directive – A Gripping Political Thriller You Can't Put Down
In the shadows of modern America, LGBTQIA+ citizens are vanishing—discreetly, efficiently, without a trace. No raids. No bar scenes. Just everyday people, taken off the streets by hooded figures claiming to be federal agents. The government denies

everything. The media stays silent. And a chilling agenda creeps forward under the radar.

When a gay investigative journalist and a tough ex-cop turned private investigator join forces, they uncover a disturbing network of data-driven surveillance, extremist influence, and a covert directive designed to erase queer lives. What begins as a mystery quickly spirals into a race against time—to expose the truth, rescue the missing, and rally a fractured community before it's too late.

If you loved *The Handmaid's Tale* or *V for Vendetta*, prepare for a bold, timely, and unforgettable new voice.
The Shadow Directive is not just a thriller—it's a wake-up call.

Divided We Fall
What happens when the truth is no longer enough—and stories are all that's left to fight tyranny? *Divided We Fall: Operation Neverland* is a cerebral, thrilling, and audacious entry in the anthology that imagines a near-future America spiraling into authoritarianism. In this mind-bending tale, a covert trio of operatives weaponizes nostalgia itself, planting psychological triggers into beloved animated classics to unravel the fractured psyche of a dangerously unstable president. As the fairy tales roll, reality bends—and democracy itself teeters on the edge of madness.

Told through shifting perspectives—covert agents, a crumbling commander-in-chief, and the unknowing family members caught in the crossfire—this short story is both dystopian satire and a cautionary tale.

Author B. Alan Bourgeois doesn't just hold a mirror to society; he shatters it and shows us what's behind the glass. With echoes of Orwell, *Black Mirror*, and political theater, *Operation Neverland* asks an unshakable question: If perception shapes power, who gets to tell the tale?

Echoes of Tomorrow: Stories of Resistance and Renewal
In *Echoes of Tomorrow: Stories of Resistance and Renewal*, a diverse tapestry of short stories weaves together themes of hope, resilience, and the unyielding human spirit. From dystopian futures marked by political unrest to deeply personal journeys of defiance and redemption, this anthology delves into the shadows of societal collapse and the light of collective transformation. With characters who stand against oppression, question entrenched systems, and inspire revolutionary change, these stories challenge readers to reflect on the precarious balance of justice, power, and humanity. A must-read for those who dream of building a brighter tomorrow.

***Texas Authors Museum & Institute of History, Award-Winning* Humanities Series**

Shattered Promises: Unveiling the Roots of Civil Unrest in America and the Path to Change
Book 1 of 3
The Humanities Series

"Shattered Promises: Unveiling the Roots of Civil Unrest in America and the Path to Change" explores the historical and contemporary forces driving civil unrest in the United States, examining the interplay of social inequality, racial and ethnic tensions, labor struggles, and government responses. With detailed analysis and historical insights, it highlights persistent disparities and challenges readers to consider whether the nation faces a turning point or revolution. Offering six actionable steps to foster equity and justice—addressing socioeconomic gaps, combating prejudice, protecting civil rights, improving government responses, promoting historical awareness, and strengthening communities—the book inspires collective action toward a fairer and more unified society.

I Know Me: You Keep Guessing
Book 2 of 3
The Humanities
Series

Discover "I Know Me: You Keep Guessing," a book that celebrates authenticity, diversity, and self-acceptance while standing against hate and discrimination. Dive into an inspiring journey of personal growth rooted in non-violence and influenced by figures like Gandhi and Jesus. Join the movement, educate yourself, and advocate for peace while spreading awareness and supporting inclusivity. Get your copy today and be part of a movement changing the world, one heart at a time. #IKnowMe #EmbraceDiversity #SpreadLove

**Help the Homeless Find Homes:
How the Public Can Help Reduce, and reverse Homelessness
Book 3 of 3
The Humanities Series**

Homelessness in America is a complex issue that affects millions of people each year. In this eye-opening book, we explore the ten most common reasons why people become homeless and how we can work to address them. From the lack of affordable housing to the impact of natural disasters, we delve into the root causes and provide insights on how we can create solutions. With personal stories, data-driven analysis, and actionable steps, this book is a must-read for anyone seeking to understand and tackle the issue of homelessness in America."

All books are Available at Your Favorite Bookstore

Y'all Write: A Month-Long Guide to Achieving Your Writing Goals
Unlock your creative potential with *Y'all Write: A Month of Writing Celebration and Growth*! This guide offers tips, motivation, and tools to help writers of all levels set goals, build momentum, and embrace the joy of storytelling.

Top Ten Things Successful Authors Do: Your Guide to Achieving Literary Success
Unlock the secrets to literary success with *Top Ten Things Successful Authors Do: Your Guide to Achieving Literary Success*. This essential guide provides actionable strategies to help writers build strong habits, master self-publishing, and thrive in their writing careers.

The Writer's Self-Care Guide: Top Ten Steps to Balance and Thrive
Transform your writing journey with *The Writer's Self-Care Guide: Top Ten Steps to Balance and Thrive*. This practical guide offers actionable steps to nurture your creativity, set boundaries, and achieve a balanced, fulfilling writing life.

Mastering Research: Top Ten Steps to Research Like a Pro
Elevate your writing with *Mastering Research: Top Ten Steps to Research Like a Pro*. This essential guide provides practical tools and techniques to conduct thorough, credible research and seamlessly integrate it into your work.

Character Chronicles: Crafting Depth and Consistency in Creative Projects

Bring your characters to life with *Character Chronicles: Crafting Depth and Consistency in Creative Projects*. This essential guide reveals professional techniques to develop authentic, complex characters that resonate across any creative medium.

Top Ten Keys for Successful Writing and Productivity

Unlock your writing potential with *Top Ten Keys for Successful Writing and Productivity*. This guide offers actionable strategies to build consistent habits, manage time effectively, and produce high-quality work to elevate your writing career.

Editing Essentials: Your Guide to Finding the Perfect Editor

Transform your manuscript with *Editing Essentials: Your Guide to Finding the Perfect Editor*. This guide provides practical steps to identify, evaluate, and collaborate with the ideal editor to elevate your writing.

AI-Powered Writing: Top Tools to Transform Your Craft

Revolutionize your writing with *Top Ten AI Programs Authors Should Use*. This guide explores powerful AI tools like Grammarly and Scrivener, offering practical tips to enhance creativity, productivity, and efficiency.

Unlocking the Business of Writing

Master the publishing world with *Unlocking the Business of Writing*. This essential guide provides expert advice and practical tips to build your author platform, maximize royalties, and turn your passion into a thriving career.

Top Ten Keys to Creating an Effective Book Cover
Create a book cover that captivates readers with *Top Ten Keys to Creating an Effective Book Cover*. This guide offers expert tips and practical advice on design, branding, and marketing to make your book stand out.

Mastering the Art of the Sales Pitch
Master the art of the sales pitch with *Top Ten Strategies for Authors: Mastering the Art of the Sales Pitch*. This guide provides essential strategies to captivate your audience, highlight your book's value, and drive its success.

Publishing Hurdles and How to Overcome Them
Overcome publishing challenges with *Top Ten Publishing Hurdles and How to Overcome Them*. This guide offers practical strategies and expert insights to help you navigate rejection, editing, marketing, and more to achieve your publishing dreams.

Indie Author Mastery: Overcoming Challenges and Building a Thriving Career
Thrive as an indie author with *The Indie Author Advantage: Mastering Control, Royalties, and Reach for Self-Publishing Success*. This guide offers actionable strategies to retain creative control, maximize royalties, and reach a global audience.

Mastering Amazon Publishing: A Comprehensive Guide to Success for Indie Authors

Achieve self-publishing success with *Mastering Amazon Publishing: A Comprehensive Guide to Success for Indie Authors*. This guide provides proven strategies to navigate KDP, boost visibility, and maximize earnings for your books.

Marketing Essentials for Authors: Proven Strategies to Boost Book Sales

Boost your book sales with *Top Ten Marketing Essentials for Authors: Proven Strategies to Promote Your Book*. This guide combines traditional and digital marketing tactics to help authors effectively connect with readers and turn their books into bestsellers.

Marketing Mastery: Avoiding Common Mistakes for Authors

Master book marketing with *Marketing Mastery: Avoiding Common Mistakes for Authors*. This guide offers actionable advice to help authors connect with readers, build a strong online presence, and achieve their publishing goals.

Author Brand Mastery: Building and Sustaining Your Unique Identity

Elevate your writing career with *Author Brand Mastery: A Comprehensive Guide to Building and Sustaining Your Unique Identity*. This guide provides practical steps to define your brand, build a professional presence, and connect meaningfully with your audience.

Reader Magnet: Top Strategies for Building an Engaged Reader Community

Build a loyal reader community with *Reader Magnet: Top Strategies for Building an Engaged Reader Community*. This guide offers actionable strategies to connect with readers, create exclusive content, and turn your audience into passionate advocates.

Author Platform Mastery: A Comprehensive Guide to Building, Monetizing, and Growing Your Audience

Build your literary empire with *Author Platform Mastery: A Comprehensive Guide to Building, Monetizing, and Growing Your Audience*. This essential guide offers practical strategies to define your brand, engage readers, and expand your reach.

Networking Success for Authors: Essential Strategies Guide

Achieve your literary goals with *Networking Success for Authors: Essential Strategies Guide*. This practical roadmap offers strategies to build meaningful connections, promote your work, and create a supportive community for lasting success.

Write, Publish, Market: The Ultimate Handbook for Author Success

Master the modern publishing landscape with *Write, Publish, Market: The Ultimate Handbook for Author Success*. This guide provides actionable strategies to build your author brand, attract readers, and achieve long-term success in your writing career.

Mastering Interviews: Essential Tips for Authors' Success

Excel in interviews with *Mastering Interviews: Essential Tips for Authors' Success*. This guide offers practical advice to confidently promote your work, connect with audiences, and turn every interview into a memorable success.

Mastering Event Presentations: Avoiding Common

Captivate your audience with *Mastering Event Presentations: Avoiding Common Author Mistakes*. This guide offers practical strategies to avoid pitfalls, engage your audience, and deliver impactful presentations that boost your confidence and connect with readers..

NFT and Blockchain Essentials for Authors' Success

Embrace the future of publishing with *NFT and Blockchain Essentials for Authors' Success*. This guide explains how blockchain and NFTs can protect your work, automate royalties, and expand your audience while maximizing revenue.

Mastering Self-Publishing: Overcoming Challenges for Indie Authors

Achieve self-publishing success with *Mastering Self-Publishing: Overcoming Challenges for Indie Authors*. This guide provides actionable strategies to market effectively, build credibility, and maximize your reach while turning your writing dreams into reality.

Survival Strategies for Indie Authors: Overcoming Challenges and Achieving Success

Thrive as an indie author with *Survival Strategies for Indie Authors: Overcoming Challenges and Achieving Success*. This guide provides practical advice and actionable tips to overcome obstacles, enhance your skills, and achieve your publishing goals.

Creating with Spirit: The Sacred Art of Writing and Publishing

Infuse your writing with mindfulness and purpose through *Creating with Spirit: The Sacred Art of Writing and Publishing*. This guide transforms your creative journey into a spiritual practice, empowering you to inspire readers and overcome challenges with authenticity and intention.

Empowering Authors: Top Ten Strategies for Writing Success and Career Growth
Achieve your writing dreams with *Empowering Authors: Top Ten Strategies for Writing Success and Career Growth*. This guide offers practical advice and proven strategies to build habits, refine your craft, and grow your author career with confidence.

The AI Author: Embracing the Future of Fiction
Embrace the future of storytelling with *The AI Author: Balancing Efficiency and Creativity in Fiction Writing*. This guide helps authors harness AI to boost productivity and creativity while preserving the emotional depth and artistry of their craft.

The Non-Fiction Nexus: Balancing AI and Human Insight in the Future of Writing
Elevate your non-fiction writing with *The Non-Fiction Nexus: Balancing AI and Human Insight in the Future of Writing*. This guide shows how to harness AI's efficiency while preserving the creativity and ethical judgment that make your work truly impactful.

A Step-by-Step Guide to Adapting Your Book into a Blockbuster Film.
Turn your book into a cinematic sensation with *From Page to Screen: A Step-by-Step Guide to Adapting Your Book into a Blockbuster Film*. This guide provides practical advice and industry insights to help

you navigate the adaptation process and bring your story to life on the big screen.

Unlock Your Full Potential in 2026: The Ultimate Year for Indie Authors!
Make 2026 your breakthrough year with *The Ultimate Year for Indie Authors*. This guide offers practical strategies to optimize publishing, leverage social media, and achieve unparalleled success in your indie author journey.

Beyond the Basics: Advanced Strategies for Indie Author Success
Elevate your indie publishing career with *Beyond the Basics: Advanced Strategies for Indie Author Success*. This guide offers actionable tips and strategies to diversify income, engage readers, and build a sustainable, thriving career.

Made in the USA
Coppell, TX
03 August 2025

52493758R00056